S

P9-CAM-214

Also by Juliet Madison

The Delta Girls
Sight
Sound

3 1969 02383 3899

Diversion Books
A Division of Diversion Publishing Corp.
443 Park Avenue South, Suite 1008
New York, New York 10016
www.DiversionBooks.com

This is a work of fiction. Names, characters, places and incidents either are the product of the author's imagination or are used fictitiously. Any resemblance to actual persons, living or dead, events or locales is entirely coincidental.

For more information, email info@diversionbooks.com

First Diversion Books edition January 2016.
Print ISBN: 978-1-62681-918-4
eBook ISBN: 978-1-62681-917-7

SCENT

THE DELTA GIRLS: BOOK THREE

JULIET MADISON

DIVERSIONBOOKS

To Jay.
My senses came alive the day you were born.

CHAPTER 1

The warm, smoky scent of firecrackers shot up my nose as colorful explosions embellished the sky, then dissipated into oblivion. It reminded me of candles and birthdays and parties and good times, of excitement and hope and dreams and new beginnings. But, as the drunken idiot who had set off his illegal homemade firecrackers an hour before the New Year's Eve countdown got escorted away by the police, I was reminded of something else.

It couldn't be true.

Not my father.

"You coming, Sasha?" my older sister Tamara asked. "Before they sell out of the good cupcakes?" She made an urgent gesture in an attempt to usher me along.

I shot another look back at the scraggy, long-haired dude—arms behind his back, cops gripping his wrists as he struggled and shouted. The expressions on the faces of the bulky men in uniform didn't change. Just another night for them, another New Year's Eve when they weren't out enjoying themselves with their buddies, or romancing their wives or girlfriends or boyfriends.

"Um, sorry, what?" I mumbled.

"What's up with you?" Tamara asked.

Then I could smell Serena's citrusy body spray beside me and turned to look at another of my four sisters. Serena was a triplet, along with me and Savannah. Her boyfriend Damon had bought the body spray for her for Christmas. I never thought she'd be one to wear perfume, but being with Damon had opened her up to new experiences.

"You're thinking about what Mom said, aren't you," Serena stated, her hand gently on my arm.

"Huh? No, I just got distracted. Okay, let's get something to eat!" I stepped away from Serena and smiled at Tamara, whose face lit up at the promise of a sugar rush.

Serena grasped my arm again. "Sash. C'mon, I can tell." She held my gaze and I softened.

"Maybe just a bit." I shrugged.

We stood in silence for a moment, the sounds of the laughing, chattering crowd appearing to dissipate into the air as the firecrackers had done.

"It's just…" I waved my hand loosely, as though summoning the words was too much effort for me. Which it kinda was. The words *Dad* and *criminal* just didn't seem to belong in the same sentence. "I don't believe he could have been involved in anything illegal. He wouldn't do that."

"You heard what Mom said," Savannah, the youngest triplet, piped up, releasing herself from Riley's almost surgically permanent embrace. "She wouldn't have told us if she didn't think it was true." She held out her arms. "So Dad made a silly mistake a billion years ago and has—*had*—a

8

criminal record. It wasn't like he was a bad guy, he just got caught up with the wrong crowd when he was young and got in trouble by association."

I crossed my arms. "That doesn't mean he repeated his mistakes years later, while we were little kids. Not when he had a family depending on him."

Serena stood in alliance beside me. I knew she didn't totally believe the possibility either, though she didn't always voice her thoughts.

"Yeah, but he could have gotten caught up with some dodgy types again. Once you're embroiled in a certain crowd it can be hard to escape." Savannah glanced at Serena. "Did I use *embroiled* correctly? Heard it somewhere the other day."

Serena nodded and sighed. How my youngest sister could go from discussing a serious matter to discussing the correct use of vocabulary I had no idea. Then again, it was probably her version of doing what I often did—using fun and humor to distract from feeling strong emotions. We each had our own ways of coping.

"Anyway," Savannah said, "it doesn't matter what he did. He was a good man. He loved us. It only matters that we find out what happened to him."

"I agree," said Talia, my fourth sister and Tamara's twin.

Tamara stepped forward. "Right, well tonight is not the time, unless you want to *connect* here and now and see what shows up in a premonition?" The crowded beach, the flames from the bonfire licking up toward the sky in sharp flicks. Not the ideal place to practice our powers. "Our visions haven't given us any more clues, so let's just enjoy the night and say goodbye to this crazy year."

Works for me.

Though, the niggling feeling that Mom could be onto something crawled uncomfortably up my spine.

'It could be why his ghost is not showing up, not helping you discover the truth of his disappearance. He might be ashamed of something he did that led to his death and wants to protect you girls from the reality.'

Mom's words that day haunted me at the weirdest times—when I was in the shower, in the middle of a boring science class, or even in the middle of a completely ordinary conversation with someone at school—'Did you watch *The Bachelor* last night?,' 'Yep, how cruel was Cindy? And, by the way, do you think my dad was a criminal?'

No. Unless there was solid proof, he would always be innocent in my eyes. Like I had been in his—*'My sweet, beautiful Sasha,'* he'd say with a loving smile as I paraded around the living room wearing Mom's flowing skirts and platform heels, an overload of beaded necklaces dangling down past my waist and threatening to make me topple forward. I still remembered the last time I saw him, the last time he spoke to me the night before he disappeared. *'Your beauty lights up the room,'* he'd said, when I'd asked him how I looked after dressing up again and putting on lipstick and two round smudges of blusher. I probably looked like a clown, but he only saw a princess. *'My princess,'* he'd said, as he kissed me goodnight and Mom took me to the bathroom to wash off the makeup. The spiced, woody scent of his cologne or aftershave or whatever he used followed me to the bathroom along with the comfort of his loving words. Even now, whenever I did my makeup or got all dressed up, I would swear I could smell it again. It was all I had left of him—the comforting, familiar, but fleeting scent of the man who should still be in my life. In *our* lives.

We queued near the food stall, and I turned side to side and scanned the crowd. "Where did Taylor get to?" I asked no one in particular.

"Yeah, I thought you two were headed for a midnight kiss for sure!" Savannah remarked, before she snuggled into her guy and kissed the side of his neck.

"There's still hope," I joked, giggling. Though it wasn't really a joking matter. I seriously wanted him to kiss me, and I wanted it to be tonight. Not in six months time, not next week, but tonight. My first New Year's kiss. *Ahhh...*

We'd met up earlier when the Iris Harbor festivities had begun, and he ate the rest of my hamburger as I couldn't finish it. I teased him and said 'you'll get girl germs' and he said 'good.' For some reason that made me like him even more.

"Hope he's not as bad as your first kiss." Savannah chuckled.

"Savvy!" Heat flushed my face, and I avoided the gazes of Riley and Damon. I didn't exactly wish to discuss my disastrous first kiss with a boy from our old school in front of boys from our new school. Or anyone, really.

"Bad, eh?" asked Riley, while Damon had the good sense to keep any thoughts on the matter to himself.

I shifted on the spot and swiped some hair off my face, though it slid back onto my cheek.

"Yeah," said Savannah. "She ended up with a sprained ankle."

Riley was the one chuckling now. "How does one get a sprained ankle from a kiss?"

"Oh, look, almost our turn to be served! Move forward people." I held my hands out to usher everyone forward in the line.

Savannah covered her mouth as she giggled. "Sasha got kissed behind the boys' toilets at the school's summer fair, but being the dignified young woman that she is, stepped backward at the shock of it all and tripped over a brick!"

"Oh yes, it's just hilarious. Thanks, Savvy."

Even Damon grinned widely.

I checked my watch. *C'mon, midnight, hurry up. And Taylor, too, wherever you are.*

"So why was the kiss so bad?" asked Riley. "Too soft, too firm, teeth in the way?"

Holy freaking moly, why was everyone so interested in this? I fiddled with my rose quartz bracelet, as though it might summon Taylor to my rescue to give me a much better kiss to talk about. The pale pink, circular stones encasing my wrist were supposed to enhance love in life, as Savannah had told me after she'd bought it for me.

"All of the above," I sighed. Might as well get it over with so we could move on to other less embarrassing topics of conversation. "He started out too soft and tickly, like he was afraid I'd break or something."

Savannah snorted. "Well, ya did!"

"But then his lips took on a life of their own and became like giant, slurpy, sucking machines, and my lip got cut by his teeth so I gasped and stepped back and my foot got caught between two bricks, and I reached out to hold him for support but he reached out to grab me at the same time and our arms banged together and that sent me flying backward, but my foot was still kind of trapped so my ankle twisted when I fell. There. The End. Happy now?" I planted my hands on my hips.

Savannah slapped her thigh with laughter, and Riley's grin mirrored Damon's. My other sisters had all heard this story before so they didn't seem as amused, but Savvy always found it hilarious and never failed to tease me at every available opportunity.

"Tell them his name!" Savannah exclaimed.

"Jordan."

"No, his *other* name!" She howled, slapping her thigh again.

Oh yeah. The name I had given him on explaining the disaster to my sisters when they watched me get a plaster cast at the hospital.

"Apoca-lips," I said.

"Like a zombie apoca-lips?" Riley remarked.

A laugh shot from everyone's mouth, save for mine. "Apoca-lips is coming, be afraid, be very afraid!"

I turned my head to the side and ignored Savannah.

"What's this about an apocalypse?"

I turned toward the unfamiliar voice that seemed to be accompanied by its own scent—sweet but spicy, cool but warm, smooth but textured, and…*mmm, hello*. My eyebrows rose and my gaze ran down and up the sculpted torso of the man behind the food stall. *Man*, I tell you, not *boy*. But young enough to be perfectly suitable boyfriend material for a girl my age.

"It's um…just ah…" My voice box was experiencing its own apocalypse.

"We were saying we're as hungry as zombies are for brains," Riley interjected. "So, what are we having, ladies and gent?" He surveyed the selection of cupcakes, lollipops, and cookies, while I surveyed the guy's dark, glistening eyes, and my peripheral vision took in his angled jaw and groomed sprinkling of stubble. Stubble! Like, *on purpose* stubble, not: I'm-still-going-through-puberty-and-I-don't-really-need-to-shave-yet-stubble.

My belly flip-flopped. *Taylor who?*

He picked up a cupcake and placed it on a paper plate, then squirted whipped cream into two small blobs on the plate, followed by a smooth arc under the cupcake. "I think this might make you smile?" he said, handing the smiling creation to me.

I took it, and predictably, smiled. "Thanks," I said. "Three dollars, yeah?" I noticed the price sign and rummaged in my pocket with my free hand.

"For you, let's make it one dollar," he replied.

I handed him three dollars anyway. "I think the charity needs it more than I do."

Oh geez, Sasha, are you trying to sound like Miss Humanitarian of the Year?

He gave a modest nod and accepted the money. As he served the others I put the plate down and took a photo of it, then uploaded it to my Facebook profile with the words: *Nothing like a sweet smile from a stranger.* Maybe Taylor would see it and get jealous.

"Bit of a photographer, eh?" the guy asked.

"Oh, no." I shrugged. "Just an avid sharer of every moment of my life on Facebook." I giggled. A stupid giggle, that probably made me sound about twelve years old.

"How'd it turn out? Not the best lighting around here for photos."

I held up my phone for him to see.

"Two likes on it already," he said with a smile, "I wonder

whether they're due to your popularity or the artistic merit of my creation." He winked, and my belly flip-flopped again.

"One for you, too?" he asked Tamara, who despite her insatiable hunger was the last to be served. She accepted a smiley cupcake as well, and bit into it immediately.

"Did you make these?" she asked.

He shook his head. "You can thank the *Home to Heart* charity volunteer bakers for them. I just volunteered to man the stall."

Hot. Mature. Friendly. Thoughtful. *And*, a volunteer?

Maybe I didn't need a New Year's kiss from Taylor after all. I'd be perfectly happy with a lingering smile from Cupcake Man.

I bet he doesn't kiss like an apocalypse.

I straightened up on realizing that my hormones were going crazy, and forced myself to look away for a moment.

"Thvh ghurd," Tamara mumbled as she ate, which I took to mean 'they're very good.'

"So, you don't do any baking yourself?" I asked. "I mean, generally, for yourself, or for special people in your life?" I really should learn to think before speaking like Serena did. I might as well have asked him, 'Do you have a girlfriend?'

"Nah. I don't exactly have the facilities in my college dorm, unfortunately. But if I did, I definitely *would* bake cupcakes for special people, or a special person, should one come into my life." He leaned on the counter and his biceps bulged through his firm, long-sleeved, ribbed top.

"So you're just home for the holidays?" Tamara asked, in between mouthfuls.

He nodded. "Visiting family on the outskirts of Iris Harbor. I come back here on the occasional weekend too."

Which meant I could potentially bump into him again.

I scrunched up my nose when a man brushed past me who had clearly forgotten to put deodorant on, and I moved away from the stall when other customers needed to be served. I smiled my thanks to College Dude and we all sat on the sand near the bonfire. Lara, Damon's sister, joined us. She had been deep in conversation with the pyrotechnicians about the science of firecrackers. They'd said she could do some work experience with them if she wanted, but she was tossing up between that and an opportunity at a marine-biology research lab.

As the pyramid shaped bonfire warmed our skin (and somehow we seemed no longer traumatized by seeing such large flames), we talked about the crazy stuff that had happened barely a few weeks ago—the ghosts, the near-miss at the cliff, the new insight into Dad's old life. What would the new year bring? Would our visions become stronger, our confidence stronger, and possibly, our challenges stronger too? I was both excited and petrified by the possibilities, but whenever the things that scared me popped into my mind, I'd try to think of things I was excited about instead. Ignorance was bliss.

The singers performing on the portable stage wound down their song as midnight neared, and the MC took to the microphone and cleared his throat with an amplified, gravelly gurgle that made Serena wince.

"Grab your special someone," he said, "and raise your plastic cups as we prepare to see Iris Harbor into the new year!"

I had neither the special someone nor the plastic cup. Not even a plate—I had already chucked it in the trash, after licking off all the whipped cream from the smiley face. Riley and Savannah stood side by side, arm in arm, heart in heart, and so did Damon and Serena. Lara held her camera up to the sky in readiness for the midnight fireworks display, and Talia and Tamara chatted about something as if the countdown was long gone and they were discussing what to cook for dinner on the weekend.

I fiddled with my fingers as I glanced around. *Where the hell was Taylor anyway?* My mind morphed into Serena's for a moment and I envisioned the worst possibilities—he was getting cozy with another girl, he was chatting to his buddies and pointing at me all alone and laughing, or he had tripped on a brick somewhere and sprained his ankle.

Oh, just forget about him!

I tried to distract myself by counting my blessings. Mom had this journal she wrote in called 'blessings,' where she wrote down good things that happened to her during the day, or things she was grateful for. She said it helped keep her mind off of worries and focused on what was good in life instead. She always said we should start our own journal to help us cope with our extra burdens and responsibilities. Maybe I *should* start my own this year; it could be my New Year's Resolution. One of them anyway, along with: dye my hair a really bright color, watch less TV, exercise more, start a blog, spend less, save more money, and—one thing that Mom would freak about if she knew—get a tattoo. Yep, not many people would expect *me* to want a tattoo. Not glamorous, refined, dignified Sasha! Anyway, I didn't think it was legal for people my age to get one, so it would probably have to wait until I was old enough. A simple love heart, that's all I wanted. A small, cute, intricate love heart. Maybe on my ankle, or wrist, or under my belly button. I smiled to myself as I thought of how I could draw one on with ink and trick my sisters into believing I got a real one. I could do that on the first of April this year.

"Good to see you smiling," said Talia. "Who needs guys, huh?" She slid her arm around my waist and gave me a squeeze.

She was right. I had a lot to be grateful for, and no gorgeous, popular, charming boy from a successful local business family was going to ruin my New Year's Eve.

"Ten, nine, eight, seven, six..." The MC's voice roared and the crowd echoed the countdown. With each number I tried to think of a wish...

"Five!" *Keep us all safe...*

"Four!" *Prove that Dad wasn't a criminal...*

"Three!" *Find out what happened to Dad and find his body...*

"Two!" *Let Mom find happiness again...*

"One!" *Fall in...*

Love? Was that what I really wanted? Was I too young to know true love, and destined to wait for at least a decade to pass until I had the opportunity to experience something amazing? For some reason, I craved it, longed for it; something to bind me to another so beautifully, intensely, permanently; something to fill that big gaping hole in my heart from...

I pushed aside the realization that I was trying to fill something that couldn't be filled, except with the return of my father, and that wasn't going to happen. So at the very least I ached for something to take up temporary residence and mask the sadness and loneliness beneath. Ignorance was bliss, remember?

I snapped out of my thoughts and realized that the countdown was finished, and as fireworks colored the sky everyone was already calling out "Happy New Year!" and smiling and laughing and hugging. And kissing.

I diverted my attention away from my two lucky sisters and glanced sideways, urging my eyes to look far away from the overload of happiness around me. My gaze fell on the charity food stall, but more specifically, on the eyes of College Dude. From the moment our eyes locked, I knew he had already been looking at me. Watching me. And he was smiling. A delicious, knowing smile, like he could tell I felt somehow different, the odd one out, as though he seemed to understand that. Like he was different too. Good different. Nice different. He wasn't a drunken idiot who set off illegal firecrackers, or a school boy who disappeared into the night, or a smelly old guy who forgot to use deodorant. He was a caring, interesting, intelligent guy. So what if he was a few years older? I kinda liked the idea of that, come to think of it. Why waste time with immature boys who didn't know whether they were coming or going? This guy struck me as someone who knew where he was going in life. Knew what he wanted. I didn't know his story, but I was intrigued.

Suddenly my resolve to not worry about boys collapsed, and as though my legs were possessed they walked me in the direction of the food stall. College Dude's smile grew wider, and my own smile slid smoothly into my cheeks. I didn't even know his name, but it was about time I found out.

"Sasha!"

My gaze, locked on College Dude, broke free and I turned to the voice behind me.

"I've been looking for you!" Taylor Petrenko's cute,

smiling face filled my vision, his long-ish but groomed, wavy hair shining in the moonlight. "Happy New Year!"

I was about to say a simple but restrained 'Happy New Year to you too' but he didn't give me the chance. Next thing I knew his lips were on mine, pressing perfectly and passionately, like our mouths were doing some kind of sensual Latin dance. His warm hands held my cheeks and heat spread through my body like he had ignited an inner bonfire.

Holy…

I lost sense of time and place. *Where was I? What just happened? Aren't I supposed to be annoyed with him?*

When he released me from his hold my lips tingled like tiny stars had been implanted and were twinkling in the night. Or like popping candy: sweet, bubbly, alive.

He smiled and his hand gently grazed my cheek as he stepped back. Then as the awareness of my surroundings kicked back in, a couple of boisterous guys I recognized from school came up to Taylor and slapped him on the back in that way that guys do.

"Taylor, buddy! Happy New Year!"

"Tay! The party's just getting started, let's get back to the rock! Gaz is waiting!"

Like being swept up by a rip in the ocean he was carried away into the crowd by a current of masculine energy. And like the scent of Dad's cologne that visited me sometimes like a ghost—intense for a moment, but fleeting—so too was my midnight kiss.

"Oh my God!" Savannah came up to me and gripped my wrists. "I knew it! I knew you'd get your kiss!"

My cheeks flushed warm again and I swiped hair off my

face. "Didn't think you would have noticed while you were busy enjoying your own."

"I have eyes in the back of my head, remember?" She winked. "Or inside them."

Eyes...

College Dude's eyes...

Oh crap.

I turned to look toward the food stall. He was no longer looking in my direction. He was talking to another girl. An *older* girl. A woman. She looked about twenty-five and her long blond hair trailed down her back like a waterfall. I tried to catch his gaze again, but his eyes were locked on hers. Then, he picked up a can of whipped cream and squirted creamy, frothy blobs onto a plate, followed by an arc, then handed the smiling cupcake face to her.

I'd just gotten my New Year's Kiss that I'd so desperately wanted, but for some reason all I could think about was the guy in my line of sight. And I tried to ignore the unwarranted jealousy that crept and twisted around my chest as the young woman giggled and held a hand to her heart at the plate he had given her. Here I was thinking I'd been special. That on seeing me he'd been inspired to create the smiley cupcake. But he'd probably done them for all the girls. All part of his customer service to raise money for charity.

I sniffed as a strange smell came into my awareness. Earthy, peppery, and a little damp. It wasn't unpleasant, but it wasn't a hundred percent appealing either. Like a nice smell that changes into something not nice because you got sick or had a bad experience around it, and now you associated those feelings with that smell and it makes you feel weird.

"Oh my God," said Savannah.

"I know, I know, he kissed me. You can stop being excited now," I replied.

"No, I don't mean…I mean oh my God." She cocked her head.

I turned around.

"Sasha? I *thought* it was you!" Dark skin merged with the night but there was no mistaking those eyes, or those teeth, as he grinned with enthusiasm and walked toward me. "I didn't know you were in Iris Harbor. I've just moved here! What a coincidence!"

I instinctively took a step back and hoped there were no stray bricks lying around.

Apoca-lips was back.

Happy New Year to me.

CHAPTER 2

New Year's Resolution #1: Start a blog

"You're up early," Serena said when I entered the living room at around nine a.m., sat on the couch, and opened up the laptop.

"It's the first day of my new life! I'm going to get started on my New Year's resolutions," I said with a yawn.

The sweet, comforting scent of hot chocolate woke me up a little more as Tamara emerged from the kitchen. "Most New Year's resolutions fail within the first forty-eight hours, you know."

"Not mine." I slid an assured glance her way. "But thanks for the vote of confidence."

"Is one of them have a second-chance-kiss with Apoca-lips now that he's stalked you from the city to Iris Harbor?" Tamara giggled, then took a sip from her hot chocolate and sat on the armchair.

I opened up Google and shook my head. "No."

Though I wouldn't mind another one from College Dude. I mean Taylor!

"And he's not stalking me," I added. "It's pure coincidence that his family decided to move here."

"Well, another kiss from Taylor, then. I bet." She made pouting movements with her lips and hugged her arms around herself. "Oh, Sasha, you are the woman of my dreams!"

Mind reader.

Serena laughed at Tamara's fake, deep voice, but kept her eyes on her phone as her thumbs tapped away at the screen. She was probably having one of her romantic text message exchanges with Damon. There were so many, she could probably turn it into a novel and become a bestselling author.

"Who knows?" I said suggestively. "I'm open to that. But, he can come to me, I'm not going to chase him or anything." I swished my hair off my shoulder with a flick of my head. But I *would* check his Facebook profile to see if he'd posted anything.

I clicked one of the links in my Google search, titled: *Wordpress.*

"And what about that gorgeous guy from the food stall. Hubba hubba!" Tamara pretended to faint.

"I thought you liked Leo," I said. She'd had her eye on our mysterious, brooding neighbor—Riley's brother—ever since we moved into number three Roach Place. And yet, they'd barely spoken. *We'd* barely spoken to him. Only Savannah had had much to do with him but didn't have much to tell us, except that Riley still hadn't told his brother the truth about their father's death. And about how he'd found out, that his girlfriend Savannah and her sisters were sensory psychics.

"I do. But shhh!" She turned red. Then she said, "So with Apoca-lips, Taylor, and College Dude, you might have yourself a little love triangle going on there, sis."

I chuckled. "If guys keep popping up around me it could turn into a love pentagon!"

"Ha!" Serena looked up from her phone. "Sounds like something Damon would say. I'm going to tell him." She tapped at the screen.

"Hey," I said, "What should I call my blog?"

"Well, what's the blog going to be about?" Tamara came over to peer at my screen.

"My New Year's resolutions."

She laughed. "Your New Year's resolution is to start a blog about your New Year's resolutions?"

I shrugged and grinned. "Pretty much!"

"How about Sasha's New Year's Resolutions?"

"Oh, very original," I teased. "Has to be something more exciting than that."

"What about incorporating something to do with the sense of scent?" Serena asked. Even though she appeared completely absorbed by her text conversation with Damon, the girl could focus on multiple things at once.

"Ooh, could be nice," I said. "But, I don't want to give away my secret. Our secret."

"Yeah but the fact that you're a perfume addict isn't a secret," said Tamara.

"Oh God, what is wrong with me?" I put the laptop on the coffee table and rushed into my bedroom where Savannah was still asleep, and spritzed myself with my daily dose of Fresh Fruity Blast. *There, that's better.* Though, I should probably start thinking about branching out into a different aroma or saving money for one of the expensive brand name ones. Or (I smiled, imagining the possibilities) maybe a certain someone would buy one for me as a gift! But who that certain someone could be I wasn't sure. Taylor was still on my mind, and our kiss was awesome, but my thoughts kept flashing to College Dude.

I returned to the living room where Serena was rubbing her nose, which was usually my signature body language. "I thought something wasn't quite right when you first came in," she said.

"I'm back to my usual self now." I got comfortable on the couch and an idea struck me as my body spray scent wafted around my nose. "I know!" I typed into the webpage:

sashasscentsationalnewyear.wordpress.com

Blog name available. *Yes!*

"Oh that's a good one," said Tamara, and when I informed Serena, she agreed. "Maybe you could do one called Serena's Soundsational New Year," she said, but Serena said she didn't have any New Year's resolutions, because she was constantly making goals and plans regardless of whether it was January or October or September or whenever.

I caught a whiff of salty air as the front door opened and Mom came floating in, her thick, sandy curls bouncing around her shoulders. "Ahh, what a beautiful morning, girls! Happy New Year, my darlings!" She gave each of us a kiss. "The others are still getting their beauty sleep, I suppose?" She placed her Hessian shoulder bag on the side table near the door. "Well, I think I'll go have a nap."

I giggled. Nine a.m. and the day was already half over for Mom. She had decided to see in the new year at sunrise on the beach instead of partying at the Iris Harbor New Year's Festival last night. "Did you work out your goals for the year, Mom?"

"Yep. All set. Sunrise on New Year's Day is a very powerful time to align with the transformative energies of the universe."

"Hope I'm not too late then!" I told her about my resolution plans and she thought it was a great idea to start a blog, though she warned me not to put too many personal details on there.

Mom floated off to her bedroom and shut the door. I wondered if one of her goals was to finally find out what happened to Dad and whether he *had* been involved in something bad. She seemed more willing to let things be than my sisters and I did. But she had been living with this knowledge about Dad for years, and we had only just found out about his past. Apparently he'd had no idea the guys he'd gotten caught up with for what was supposed to be a simple robbery, would be armed. An accessory to armed robbery didn't sound too good on a resume. Hence starting his own business. Mom said he'd tried to escape their grip for years and eventually forged ahead with a new life for himself and Mom, leading to having five kids and running a computer repair store.

Before my mind became bogged down with worry and uncertainty, I turned my attention back to the screen. "Oh cool! I can choose my own design and color scheme for the blog." I scrolled through the options, but most of the ones I liked the best were premium designs that required money.

Another New Year's resolution: Make some money. Somehow.

I opted for a simple design with a pale pink background and fuchsia-colored font. I set up all the basic information and then there it was: my very own blog on the internet. "First resolution, done!" I did a little wiggle in victory.

"Yeah, but you have to actually write something on your blog for it to officially be started," said Tamara.

"I wrote the title," I defended. "But okay, I'll write the first post now. Just to get the ball rolling."

I clicked 'add new post' and wrote whatever came into my mind:

> *Hello world! It's me, Sasha. Welcome to my blog.*
>
> *This blog is all about my New Year's Resolutions, and the first one has already been achieved—start a blog! Yay! Now to do the others. I will post them here and share my progress with achieving them. I already know a few things I want to do, but I'm sure I can think of others. Some will be one-off things, others will be ongoing.*
>
> *One of my sisters says that resolutions often fail. Well to that I say…not mine! At least, I will try my best. And having a blog will be a way to help me stick to my plans.*
>
> *Oh, and you might be wondering why it's called Sasha's Scentsational New Year, well, I want to have a sensational new year of course, but the spelling of the word is because I'm a bit of a perfume addict. I love beautiful scents, and I guess you could say I have a good sense of smell. This can be both a blessing and a curse. ;) So I thought it would be fun to combine the two words to make this blog more unique— more me.*

So if anyone is reading this, I hope you will find my posts kind of interesting. Feel free to leave a comment for me to wish me well (please?)!

"I'm going to tell all my Facebook friends." I opened Facebook on another browser tab instead of my phone, and logged in. "Ooh, what if my blog goes viral and I become, like, one of those famous bloggers and inspire people all over the world to live the life of their dreams! I could start a movement." I imagined myself being interviewed on television, and walking the red carpet for some kind of exclusive blogger event, and then being able to make money from ads or something on my blog because advertisers wanted to cash in on my thousands and thousands of visitors.

"Or nobody might read it except us." Tamara chuckled.

"Hey! They will, you wait and see. I might even make a Facebook page especially for it so I can get fans, not just the friends on my private account."

I copied the link to my blog and typed into Facebook:

Happy New Year! I have an announcement: I've started a blog! Would love it if you'd visit and let me know what you think, and please share the link with friends. Let's all have an awesome year!

I added about five emoticons of various types, including a party balloon, confetti, streamers, and to tie in with my theme—a bottle of perfume. I made the post a public one and clicked 'post.'

While waiting for the thousands to flock to my blog, I checked Taylor's profile. He hadn't posted anything since before the festival last night, though a friend had tagged him in a photo where he and a couple of his friends were standing at the top of the large rock on the beach, arms raised high in victory like they'd climbed Mount Everest. The sight of his cute smile made a little butterfly take residence in my stomach. Not a nervous one, an excited one.

Those lips kissed mine last night!

I wondered whether to send him a message. Or maybe I should just wait until school started again on Wednesday. Was the kiss just a random New Year's kiss in the excitement of the night? Or did it mean he wanted to start something with me?

A notification popped up that a friend had clicked 'like' on my post. I refreshed my blog page and saw a comment that needed approval. It was from one of my friends from my old school back in the city.

Good luck Sasha! Cool idea! she commented.

"And so it begins," I said, turning to Tamara with a smug grin.

I glanced back at the screen and returned to Facebook, only then noticing the little red flag on the friend request icon. *Gee, popular me.*

I clicked it and bit the corner of my lip. *Hmm, to friend or not to friend…*

It was Jordan Davis.

Apoca-lips.

CHAPTER 3

One day down, three hundred sixty four to go. Was that really all we had? Hours to make up each day, days to make up each week, weeks to make months, and months to make a year. And then, bam!—another year gone by. Another year without Dad, another year without answers. Not this year. Something told me this year would be different. This year felt urgent, important, significant. And not only because I'd be turning seventeen, which I couldn't wait for—sixteen sounded so young. But I didn't feel sixteen, I felt seventeen, or even eighteen. Hard to believe that in just over three years I'd be twenty, along with Savannah and Serena. Twenty. Now *that* sounded old.

I wonder if that's how old College Dude is. He looks about twenty.

And there we go again, some random stranger I'd said only a few words to was gatecrashing my thoughts. I blamed hormones. They made me think, and *feel*, weird stuff. He probably wouldn't be interested in me anyway, I was too young. Sixteen and all that. Yep. I would turn all thoughts back to Taylor. He was my age. I could imagine us being twenty together, taking over his family business, whatever it was that his parents did. Something to do with investing. Or insurance. Or investing in insurance. Money stuff, anyway. Of course, I would have to find something not boring to do in the business, or in other words, not the insurance or investing stuff, but something else fun. Like decorating the office, organizing business travel arrangements, or handling clients with my charm and wit. I had charm and wit, didn't I? If I didn't I would just pretend I did. Fake it 'til you make it, or so they say.

"Coming, Sash?" asked Savannah.

It was time for our after dinner *connecting* session. But I was back on the computer, replying to a couple of new comments left on my blog. "In a sec!" All the comments were from people I knew, except one from someone called *modernprophet*, saying: *Great idea for a blog, good luck!* Who was that? I didn't know anyone who could potentially be a 'modern prophet.' I clicked on the hyperlinked username and it opened to someone's blog. Oh, maybe other bloggers somehow got notified of new bloggers, and I would start interacting with other bloggers around the world and make new online friends.

I was about to read what the blog was about when a notification popped up on Facebook. I wondered if because I had decided to accept Jordan's friend request that maybe it was him, and I dreaded the possibility, however unlikely, that he would post something like this to my wall for all to see:

Thanks for friending me Sasha! Just wanted to apologize again for kissing you so disastrously and causing you to sprain your ankle. I promise it won't happen again. The sprained ankle, not the kiss.

*Because the kiss, that can totally happen again, if you want it to?
What do you say? My lips are ready when you are.*

Yours lovingly, Apoca-lips.

Except, he wouldn't sign it *Apoca-lips* because he wasn't aware I called him that, and he would never find out. I hoped. I felt kind of bad calling him that now that he was here in town and no longer just a memory. It had been a silly mistake in a moment of hormonal overload. I *had* liked him—he was sweet, though slightly awkward at times, but after the kiss, well, I couldn't look at him the same way again.

My heart fluttered when I saw that Taylor had liked my status update, the one about my new blog. Did that mean he'd read the blog post? I refreshed the page to check for new comments but there were none. A moment later, another notification popped up. My eyes widened. Taylor had commented on my Facebook status:

How good was the NYE festival last night!

The festival, or the kiss? My fingers hovered over the keys. Should I just click like or reply to his comment? I didn't want to seem too keen but didn't want to ignore his comment either. I bit my bottom lip then typed:

It was an awesome night! Then I backspaced and changed awesome to *great*.

I chuckled to myself when I wondered what would happen if in an alternate world I had typed:

It was a great night! Especially our kiss at midnight. Oh Taylor, you are like popping candy to my heart: sweet, surprising, and totally addictive! Can we do it again? My lips are ready when you are.

Then I realized it would have sounded like the female version of the fictional Apoca-lips comment. God, I was cheesy. Luckily I didn't share the cheese with anyone in public, it stayed in my mind where it belonged. I had tried to write poetry once, but my attempts had ended up in the trash along with my self-confidence. I sucked at it, big time. But I wished I didn't, there was something about how words could be strung together beautifully that appealed to me, made me feel a sense of wonder and excitement about life and how emotions could be expressed so accurately in only a few written words. By people that didn't suck at poetry, that was.

Aha! I held up my finger. Another resolution idea: try again to write a poem. One that didn't completely suck. And I would try extra hard because I would have to post it on my blog. Maybe if I knew that people were going to read it I'd do a better job. But I wouldn't try yet, there were a few other resolutions to get through first. Like tomorrow's: dye my hair. It was the last day before school started back up, so I wanted to do it while I had the time.

"Are you writing more resolutions on your blog?" Savannah asked.

"Not yet, just thinking about tomorrow's resolution fulfillment. What color should I dye my hair?" I asked, running my hands down my brown hair, though I already knew the answer. I just wanted to see what crazy suggestion Savannah would come up with.

"Gray. You always say you want to be older and wiser." She winked.

I gave her an 'are you kidding me?' look. "I will never have gray hair. Even when I'm old and it starts going gray. I'll kill those nasty little suckers with chemicals before they get a chance to take hold." I gave a sharp nod. "I'm going to dye it a sort of burgundy crimson, know what I mean?"

34

"Like purply-red?"

"Yeah, see?" I opened a webpage and showed her the search results. It would be perfect for my dark hair, and I could wear lipstick and nail polish to match. I couldn't wait. "I'll pick up a hair dye kit from the store tomorrow."

"What would I look like as a blond?" Savvy asked, swiping her hair in an arc across her forehead.

"Crappy. Sorry." I shrugged.

"It's okay. I agree, I wasn't being serious." She blew her hair off her forehead with a puff of air from her mouth and left the room, her voice calling back, "When you're ready, Miss Scentsational."

Oh yeah. Time to connect.

If only I could write a blog about our visions. An anonymous blog. But I couldn't risk it. We had our vision journal for that, and it was for our eyes only.

I closed the laptop and met my sisters in the bedroom, hands at the ready. My chest tightened at the anticipation. Maybe this time we'd sense something to do with Dad. We hadn't yet, even though Mom had told us about the criminal record. A twinge of doubt twisted into a knot in my stomach. Doubting myself and my belief in my dad. Maybe it was possible that Mom was right, and Dad wasn't giving us any information because he truly was ashamed of what he'd done. Whatever that may be.

We held hands and closed our eyes, and the familiar jolt enlivened my body. It no longer shocked me, or any of us; it just sparked something inside of us and triggered the onset of the bubbly sensation. And then the waiting. Sometimes the smells would come instantly, other times there'd be nothing for a few minutes and then something would shoot up my nose in a flash, metaphorically speaking. I breathed slowly and deeply, ready to catch a whiff of whatever the future held. Sometimes it felt weird, being able to smell the future. I mean, what kind of ability was that? If it weren't for my sisters I'd be clueless about what any of it meant. We needed each of the five senses to figure out the predictions. Together we were one body, one brain. Without them, what I sensed were just random smells. And sometimes they were gross.

What is that?

Something chemical, or dirty smelling. Like being at a mechanic shop or an old garage or something. For a moment it made me think of Wayne, the mechanic who'd dated Mom. I sucked in a deep breath and shook the memory away. It wouldn't be about him, he was no longer in our lives.

The scent disappeared like a gush of wind had taken it hostage. Then a new one took its place...*Oh. Oh wow*...It was stronger than usual, deeper and more textured than I'd experienced before. Warm, woody, earthy, with a tingle of spice. It comforted me like the gentle flickering of a candle, the way a warm fireplace in winter would have done before the events of last year at Mom's play. Though fire no longer scared me, it still held a sense of something. Uncertainty? It was both a comfort and a warning to me now. But now, with this familiar scent filling my awareness, it made me think only of the times during childhood when as a family we'd gather around the fireplace and toast marshmallows.

Dad's cologne. One smell. A smell that was probably not unique to him, I mean, any other man could wear the same cologne, but to me—it was his signature. His scent. It told me he was somehow still around, still looking out for us.

And as I breathed it in like I'd been underwater and it was my oxygen, I didn't want it to go away. Didn't want that gush of wind to take it hostage too. To take the only thing I had left of my Dad.

Savannah's hand dropped away suddenly from mine. "God! Wish I hadn't seen that."

I opened my eyes and looked at my sister. Her face was squished like she'd seen something getting, well, *squished*. "What did you see?"

"A rock, the size of my hand. It was used as a weapon."

"A weapon?" I asked.

"Oh," said Talia. "That's what I felt then. Lumpy, hard rock in my hand, and then it banged against something."

Serena shivered and her face went pale. Paler than her usual pale. "Don't tell me what I heard was the rock against someone's…"

"Head, yes," said Savannah.

Serena slumped on her bed with her face in her hands. "Why do we always see stuff like this? Bad stuff? I wish we could get a break from it for a change."

We *had* had a break, a short one at least. And as much as I agreed with her, there was no denying that our visions were important, and had helped save a life before Christmas. Like it or not, for some reason we had been chosen to receive this gift, and all the challenges that went along with it.

"Did you see who, Savvy?" I asked, deciding not to mention the presence of Dad's cologne yet.

Was it him? Was it Dad who had been hit on the head with a rock? I didn't even want to imagine it, but at the same time, if it meant finding out the truth about him, we had to stay open to the possibility.

She scrunched up her eyes. "It was really dark. I think it was a man. Or a woman with short hair. Dark hair too, or maybe he wasn't and it was just because it was nighttime."

"The rock felt big in my hand, like I could only just get a handle on it, I had to grip it really tightly so I wouldn't lose hold," said Talia.

"I think the person holding the rock, the one who…"

Hurt, or possibly…killed someone…

"Well, I think it was a female hand. I can't be totally sure though." Savannah held her hand in front of her and rotated it around, like she was trying to remember what it looked like as it had held the rock. "Maybe the large rock just made the hand look small." She shrugged.

I glanced at Tamara, who was silent. "I'm guessing you didn't really taste anything for this one?" I asked.

She shifted on the spot and twisted her lips to one side. "I did, actually. I tasted blood." She shivered too and sat next to Serena. "I don't get what those vampires think is so good about it." She attempted a chuckle, but gulped.

It was usually me saying things like that, but I couldn't think of any jokes at the moment. I wanted to go back in the vision and smell Dad's cologne again, let it wrap itself around me like a soft blanket until I fell asleep, smiling. "So you didn't see Dad?" I blurted, and Savannah's eyes bulged.

"No, why?" She stepped closer to me and looked me in the eye. "Was he in your vision? Did you smell something?"

"His cologne." Saying it out loud made me feel all wobbly and weak. I sat on the bed too, scared that if I didn't I would lose balance and fall over as though the gush of wind had decided not to take me hostage but knock me down with its intensity.

"Oh, wow." Talia put a hand on my shoulder. "I wish I could smell it."

I didn't. I mean, *I* wanted to smell it, but I didn't wish it on Talia. She probably wouldn't be able to handle it. Though she was like the protector, the guide out of all of us with her clear thinking and decision making skills, she felt things so deeply, so strongly, that I was sure she'd be too sensitive to cope.

I stood. "Anyway, so let's write this down, yeah?" If I dwelled on the scent and the emotions accompanying it I feared I would get washed away and lose my grip on the present moment, the here and now. Reality.

Talia got out the journal. Serena had originally been the one to write everything down, but somehow, and I don't recall when it had started, Talia had taken over. She was able to write really quickly now, her hands moved like lightning across the page, and I could smell the ink as it rolled from the pen and marked its territory on the paper.

Dad's cologne…

A rock…

A hand…

A weapon…

A thud, a crack…

Blood…

"We should try again," said Savannah. "I pulled us out of the vision too quickly. I was shocked, that's all. But I'm ready now. I want to see more." She held out her hands.

We formed a circle and connected, and I closed my eyes and waited. Waited for Dad to visit me again, for his scent to waft around me and bring me peace. Maybe the smell had simply been his way of telling me I was right. That he hadn't been involved in anything bad. That I shouldn't listen to what anyone else said, no matter what his past may lead us to believe.

But he didn't come. A hole gaped in my heart, and I longed to release my sisters' hands and do something to distract myself from the disappointment. But another smell manifested. A chemical smell, but not like the garage or mechanic one before.

Savvy laughed and dropped her hands. I shot a glance her way. She looked at me and giggled. "Oh dear," she said. "Sasha, I strongly advise against you buying a hair dye kit tomorrow."

"Is that why I heard Sasha crying in despair like it was the end of the world?" asked Serena.

"Huh? What do you mean?" I crossed my arms. "Was that hair dye that I could smell?" It made sense now. The chemicals.

"Yep, but I think you got a dodgy kit. You shouldn't try to do two resolutions in one—save money *and* dye your hair." She giggled again. "It turned out patchy, and was more like a burnt orangey purple color if that's even possible. You looked like you'd rolled around in some kind of red dirt and then tipped crushed blueberries on your head."

Tamara snorted with laughter, my sisters giggled, and my mouth gaped. "No way! Oh my God. What am I going to do? Should I just buy the more expensive kit?"

"If you could have seen what I saw, you wouldn't want to risk it," Savannah said. "I think you should get a professional to do it."

"But that's going to use up all my spare cash."

"We have this gift for a reason, remember?" She held up

her hands as though I could take it or leave it. "Blueberry dirt head or burgundy crimson, your choice."

I didn't know if I could get a hairdresser's appointment on such short notice, especially right after New Year's, but I would get up extra early and call first thing to see if I could book it. When it came to my hair, or any part of me visible to the public, I wouldn't take the risk. It would have to be a job for the professionals.

As Talia and Tamara left the room, and Serena tapped away at her phone, and Savannah did her nightly stretches, I thought about Dad's cologne and his secret past. I thought about the rock weapon, and about Taylor, Apoca-lips, and College Dude. I thought about the three hundred sixty four days left of this important year, and wished I had a professional I could call on to help me make sure that each and every one of them counted. That each day would bring me closer to my goals, closer to the truth, and closer to closure. But there wasn't one. The only person I could call on, apart from my sisters, was myself. It was up to me to make this year what I wanted. I didn't know where I'd be this time next year, but I hoped, *wished*, with all my heart and soul, that all that concerned me right here and now would be long gone, swept away in that gust of wind, never to worry me again.

CHAPTER 4

New Year's Resolution #2: Dye my hair

"Ta-da!" I smoothed my hands down my hair. Savannah and Riley sat on top of a picnic table in the park by the harbor. Rebels.

Savannah's eyes widened. "It looks freaking awesome!" She leapt off the table and touched my sleek burgundy-crimson strands. "So glad—I was worried you'd turn up looking like the disaster from my vision!"

"More visions?" asked Riley. "You didn't tell me."

The poor guy sometimes felt left out, I thought. His girlfriend and her sisters practically had superpowers and he was just…Riley. So he was fit as hell but could he predict the future? No. Heck, sometimes I didn't even know if *we* could do it that well. We'd had successes, but a lot of the time it felt like we were fumbling around in the dark searching for the light switch.

Savvy flicked her hand. "Oh, I just helped Sasha avoid a potential hair catastrophe."

And saw someone get whacked on the head with a rock, by the way, in case you were wondering.

I never knew how much Savannah told Riley. She was pretty open with him, but for some reason she obviously hadn't told him about the vision. Maybe she was worried that if it was our Dad who'd been hurt—*killed*—in that way, it would open up the floodgates to a whole lot of stuff they didn't want to revisit. Riley too, because of his own dad's death.

"Good to know your powers are making such a huge difference in the world," Riley teased, winking at me. "Looks good, Sash," he said.

"Thanks." I smiled.

"You gonna come with us to the movies?" Savannah asked.

"What, now?"

"Yeah, Serena and Damon too. Not Lara though, she's apparently writing up her schedule for the year."

Hmm, movies with two sets of lovebirds?

"Nah, I'm going to go home and work on my blog now that resolution number two has been completed. Thanks though."

"You're really getting into this blogging thing aren't you?"

"The blogging is just a way for me to express myself and keep on track. It's the resolutions that I'm getting into." I gave a nod.

"What's next? Climb Mount Everest?" Riley asked, and I'm sure if I'd said yes he would say something like 'race you to the top!' and start his expedition immediately. Savannah would say 'wait up!' and then they would both make it to the top with barely any sweat and I'd probably still be stuck at the bottom because I was worried I wouldn't get reception at the top to check my Facebook notifications. Or blog comments. Priorities, right?

"Maybe next year," I chuckled. "See you later."

I walked off and turned back briefly, smiling at how Riley and Savannah were pretend punching each other. Riley held up an arm to block her attack and then grabbed her hands and pulled her in close for a kiss. He'd been teaching her some Taekwondo skills over the holiday break, and she was going to start proper classes this week. They could be each other's bodyguards.

The afternoon breeze picked up and whooshed past me as I walked up Luxford Street, salt and sea smells filling my nose. I silently thanked Mother Nature that it wasn't going the other direction and whooshing my hair forward, messing up the hairdresser's handiwork. Still, I might need to touch up the look with some hair serum when I got home.

I was about to cross the road into Roach Place when the smell of car fumes made me stop. I could always smell things before I could see or hear them. Good thing too, because right after I stopped, a vehicle sped past me and careened around the sharp curve of the road where Luxford Street met Roach Place. I turned my head to the left and watched the black pickup truck zoom down the street. It was polished, glossy like oil, and I doubted the truck was used for anything practical but simply to look good. And masculine. *Idiot.*

Someone was standing on his front lawn watching

the truck. Then he turned in my direction and our distant gazes met.

Jordan waved. A feeble, uncertain, please-don't-hate-me wave. Unless I was wrong and it was a what-the-hell-have-you-done-to-your-hair wave. Of course I didn't hate him, I just associated him with feelings of awkwardness and inexperience. Both from him, and myself. I felt embarrassed around him. But as he waved, I realized for the first time that he probably felt more embarrassed than me. If it wasn't for his apocalyptic kissing attempt I wouldn't have tripped in the first place. And despite his apparent confidence when he saw me on New Year's Eve, deep down he was probably not only humiliated with a capital H but with *all* capitals. Like caps lock humiliated. HUMILIATED.

Poor dude.

I waved back—a subtle, yet certain, it's-okay-I-don't-hate-you-I'm-just-embarrassed wave. His smile widened and he slipped his hands into his pockets, then turned to go back inside his house.

Geez, this *was* a small town. First, we moved in next door to our science teacher, then Savannah hooked up with our hot, sporty neighbor (i.e., her soulmate), Taylor lived further down Luxford Street (and yes, I did discreetly peek at the windows when I went past a few minutes before, and no, he didn't seem to be there), and now, Jordan Davis lived just down the road from me, in the L curve of Luxford Street. Who would join the neighborhood party next? College Dude?

I walked past Mr. Jenkins's house (who was probably busy planning his science lessons) and up to number three. Home. My home. Our home. Or was it really? It, and our previous house, had never really felt like home since Dad disappeared, more like we were staying in a motel or budget holiday rental. There was always this sense of something missing, not quite right, a void in the air around us like a porthole to a dark, desperate world where no one ever returned. *It* was always present, unlike him. That gaping, vacuum of nothingness that tempted us, told us we could just fall into it and surrender to the Not Knowing, let it engulf and embody us so that we never thought about Dad again, and just lived out our monotonous existence day to day, moving forward but staying still at the same time.

It would be both the easiest and hardest thing to do. Just let go, let it all go, and get on with our lives. No more worry, no more pressure. But that would mean giving up. And forgetting. And that just wasn't right.

No. It wouldn't win.

We would win. Somehow, sometime, we would win.

We had to.

I rushed into the bathroom when I got home and touched up my lipstick, pressing my lips together.

C'mon, Dad, are you here?

I patted translucent powder on my nose, matteifying (my own made up word—clever me) the sheen.

Do you like my new hair, Dad?

I breathed in deeply, waiting for the scent, the spice, the warm comforting aroma to embrace me like his arms no longer could.

I squirted some hair-smoothing serum into my palm and rubbed my hands together, then spread it over my slightly windswept hair. When I placed it back on the crowded wall shelf, a few bottles fell off. One with a loud smash, which I was sure Serena could hear from all the way in town where she was having the World's Best Hot Chocolate with Damon at a café.

"Damn!" I jumped back, trying to avoid tiny glass shards launching themselves into my skin. The lid of a tube of Talia's hand cream had come off, and thick cream covered the floor.

Talia yanked open the bathroom door. "What happened?" She eyed the mess. "Oh, that cream was new!" She tried to scoop as much of it up as she could and back into the tube, but because there were also glass fragments on the floor she gave up and chucked it in the trash.

"I guess you don't want to turn it into a revolutionary new hand cream with exfoliating, skin refining glass shards?" I asked, hunching my shoulders.

She sighed, then looked at the shelf. "Seriously, you need to throw out some of this stuff and make room for our things too." She pointed to a couple of my many bottles of various cosmetics and hair items. "I mean, do you really need hair smoothing serum *and* hair curling cream? And what on earth is skin primer?"

I crossed my arms. "Yes. I do, in fact. Sometimes I like straight hair and sometimes I like my natural waves. There's nothing wrong with variety. And as for skin primer—"

"I don't really want to know what skin primer is, let's just get this stuff cleaned up." She sighed again and bent down, picking up a couple of large chunks of broken bottle with the tips of her fingers. "Well, go get some newspaper and a dustpan and a plastic bag!"

"Yes, *Mom*," I teased. Though she didn't really sound like Mom. Mom would be more like, 'Oh, whoopsie! Never you mind, it's only a bit of broken glass, we'll get this cleaned up in no time. It will even give us a chance to have some mother daughter bonding time! See? What a gift some challenges can be. A blessing.'

Blessings. That could be my next resolution: start my Blessings Journal. After I posted about my hair.

Talia and I cleaned up the bathroom, then I sat on the couch and opened the laptop, a flicker of relief washing over me that the bathroom incident had at least distracted me from the fact that I hadn't been able to smell Dad's cologne. That he hadn't *visited* me.

Maybe he *was* ashamed…

Stop it! I ignored the little voice in my mind and opened up my blog.

Oh! Almost forgot. I picked up my phone and held it in front of me and snapped a selfie. I didn't like the result though so I took another, and then another, until six photos later I was happy enough with what would be my 'after' photo and my new Facebook profile pic.

I did it! I dyed my hair. Resolution number two—done, baby!

I wrote my blog post and inserted a before and after photo. Then I copied the link to the post and put it in a Facebook status. After that I updated my profile picture and watched as likes and comments appeared.

Nice!

Gorgeous color!

OMG I want hair like that!

You look so hot!

Wait—who said that? Oh, that's right, it was just my imagination pretending Taylor had left a comment. I giggled to myself.

Mom came out from her bedroom where she had been having another nap. "I think I overslept. Looks like I'll be up late tonight, sweeties." She kissed the top of my head and then Talia's.

"What time do you start back at work tomorrow?" Talia asked.

"Eight a.m. So I'll need you girls to lock up when you leave, please. Unless you want to get to school before I go and start your learning adventures bright and early?" she joked.

"Um, nope," I said. "But, I do want to start something else." I looked up at Mom. "Do you have a spare journal I could have? I forgot to buy one today."

Mom's eyes widened. "A journal? Are you going to start a..." She moved her hand in circles, waiting for me to tell her what she hoped to hear.

"A Blessings Journal, yes." I smiled.

Mom clasped her hands together. "Oh, goodie!" She dashed into her room and returned a moment later with a hard cover notebook. She placed it in my hands like it was the key to world peace, and the scent of fresh, crisp paper wafted up to my nose, waiting for me to fill its pages with words and thoughts in physical form. On the cover was an illustration of an empowered looking woman, though she was abstract and fluid and appeared to be merging with her surroundings. "She's a representation of your inner warrior, my darling. You have more strength inside you than you realize. And as you write your blessings, you'll grow and become even stronger." She kissed my head again. I pretended to do some sort of ninja move with my hands and made a 'hiy-ah!' sound. Mom laughed and went to the kitchen, mumbling with enthusiasm, "Ooh, wonder if it's too early for a little teensy bit of wine..."

"I'll have some!" I called out.

Mom stuck her head around the corner with an exaggerated glare. "I don't think so, young lady." She smiled and her head disappeared from view.

Disappeared.

Dad disappeared.

Head.

Hit with a rock.

Vision—past or future?

I shivered, wishing I could stop some of the random thoughts and images that invaded my mind sometimes.

Push them away, push them away...

I needed a distraction. My fingers tapped on the notebook and I opened it. May the Blessings Journal begin! I grabbed a pen from the coffee table where it was resting on a half completed crossword puzzle, which I assumed to be either Mom's or Serena's, and wrote today's date on the first page.

Okay, what am I grateful for?

I pondered my life and the day's events.

My new hair? But that sounded silly and self-centered.

I thought about all the basics like food, water, oxygen, a roof over our head, but that went without saying. Surely I could come up with something more unique to me, something more exciting to start off this journal with a big 'woohoo!'?

I closed the notebook, deciding not to rush it.

The front door opened and a rosy-cheeked Tamara walked in. "Guess who I bumped into down at the harbor?" She grinned. "*And,* guess who said to say 'hi' to you?" She eyed me with a suggestive, flirty look.

A smile tickled the corner of my lips.

Hmm, maybe I *would* have something good to write down as my first blessing for the year.

CHAPTER 5

It was ironic that while one of my resolutions was to attempt writing a poem, we would be studying poetry in English class with Miss Weir. Or, *Miss Weird*, as some of the students liked to call her behind her back (not me of course, I preferred Miss Weirdo).

I wasn't convinced that the classes would help with my own literary explorations. Poetry only sounded good if you were from the nineteenth century, when people used words like *thy* and *thou* and what else? Oh yes—*alas! Alas, thy shalt not become thou great poet.*

Oh well. Sucks to be me.

Actually, it didn't *totally* suck to be me. College Dude had said to say 'hi' to me via Tamara yesterday. She said he'd been sitting on the pier eating a hamburger, his legs dangling over the edge, pondering his own life, so he'd told her. I couldn't imagine Taylor pondering his own life, he was too busy living it. But there was something alluring about a boy, oh excuse me—a *man*, taking time to think and ponder stuff.

In fact, I had decided that after school today I would take a walk down to the harbor myself and do a bit of pondering. Maybe I would bump into College Dude too and I would get to find out his name. We would wander yonder and ponder whilst growing fonder of each other. Huh. Maybe I *could* be a poet. Or at least think up stuff that rhymed.

But Taylor…oh, Taylor, how I adore thee! How your eyes do hypnotize me with their…with their…oh crap, what do they hypnotize me with? Yeah, *so* not a poet.

"Sasha! I asked what do you think is responsible for the transformation in the author's emotional state from hopeful to hopeless by the end of the poem?" Miss Weirdo brought me back to the present. Her beady eyes stared like tiny deadly bugs through her oversized glasses that needed a good defogging. If I didn't answer soon I could just imagine the little critters leaping out from her eye sockets, smashing through the glass lenses and catapulting themselves toward me to inflict microscopic torture until I formulated an articulate, thoughtful response.

Why did teachers always like to put students on the spot? I caught Taylor's gaze, his head turned to face me from the seat diagonally opposite.

Help! I silently urged with my eyes. But he shrugged discreetly.

"Umm…" I pretended I was getting ready to answer, when Apoca-lips, I mean *Jordan* (I really should give up the nicknames for people and be a nicer person), who was seated in front of me, cleared his throat and pretended to scratch the back of his shoulder. In his hand was a scrap of paper with the words: *self doubt triggered by his brother's offhand remark.*

I sat up straight. "Um, it was when his brother, um, said

that thing, and it made the author doubt himself, like, all his old crap from the past came up, and, oops sorry, his old *challenges* came up again, in his mind. So it was the doubt. The self doubt. Thanks to the brother dude who should have kept his big mouth shut."

As *I* should have, by this point.

Taylor grinned and gave me a thumbs up. Jordan removed the paper and stopped pretend-scratching his shoulder.

Miss Weir gave a couple of slow nods like she was pondering my answer, or trying to get her mind to translate it into a language she could comprehend. Like nineteenth century English. Her tight, wiry curls appeared to vibrate as she nodded, and while I waited for a response I amused myself by imagining there were also little beady bugs trapped in her maze of gray hair, weaving their way through the rigid curls and trying to escape. One would reach the top of her head and jump off in victory, only to land on a sharp, wiry curl that had a split end because she obviously didn't use hair smoothing serum or curl cream (take that Talia!), and the poor little bug would become impaled by the strand of hair and be left alone to die a painful death, forever trapped on the English teacher's head. All the other bugs would bow below it in honor; the one, courageous bug who came so close to escape, and would now leave a legacy of—

"I believe your answer is correct, Sasha." Miss Weir's response broke my insane thoughts and I was vaguely annoyed that my amusing fantasy could not continue. Maybe I was more Miss Weirdo than she was.

I tapped my foot against the back of Jordan's chair and he leaned back a little. "Thanks," I whispered to the back of his dark, closely-shaven head.

He leaned on his desk, then back again and scratched his shoulder, but on the piece of paper it said: *my pleasure*.

Maybe the awkwardness between us was starting to fade away.

Maybe...

After class when I got my bag from my locker and was checking my phone, I turned to walk down the hall but bumped into Jordan. Well, *he* bumped into me. He was looking at his phone too. Mine slipped from my grasp and landed first on my foot, then on the floor.

"Oops, sorry!" He bent down and picked it up for me. "Lucky it landed on your foot first, otherwise the screen could have smashed."

Like, lucky the brick had been there that day of the kiss?

"Yeah, I really should get a protective cover sometime," I replied, then noticed Taylor was half-looking in his nearby locker and half-looking at Jordan and me. "Hey, thanks for helping me out in there." I cocked my head toward the classroom.

"No problem. I had an itchy shoulder anyway so I figured I'd kill two birds with one stone." He smiled.

"Make sure you sit in front of me again next time, just in case," I joked. Though I meant it. "And if your shoulder is itchy again feel free to scratch it."

In my peripheral vision I could see that Taylor looked confused. He was also taking a super-long time to get his stuff out of his locker.

"Happy to help." Jordan scratched his head. Perhaps his shoulder itch had migrated north. "Um, your hair looks good by the way. Nice and purple. I mean, sort of reddish purple, like an exotic flower or something." He adjusted his backpack strap over his shoulder. "I would have said so yesterday when you walked past, but you were too far away and I thought it would be a bit weird to yell out, YOUR HAIR LOOKS GOOD, SASHA!" he raised his voice, and then dropped his gaze a little as though he regretted saying it.

"Um, thanks," I replied, instinctively tucking my hair behind my ear. Then I moved it back in front of my ear. My straightened hair didn't look good behind my ears, made me look like an elf from *Lord of the Rings* or something.

Taylor closed his locker with a firm clang and Jordan briefly turned to the noise. I thought Taylor would walk off but he just stood there, facing his closed locker, doing something with his phone.

Jordan raised his eyebrows. "So, do you live on Luxford Street too?"

"No, just around the corner in Roach Place. Number three."

Why did I give him my address? Maybe I subconsciously wanted Taylor to hear. I was sure he knew I was somewhere in the vicinity of Roach Place though, as I walked past his house further down Luxford Street each day, and it only led to a few other streets.

"Do you get a lot of roaches?" He did that dropped gaze thing again. Poor dude was trying too hard. It was kind of cute, and his little remarks like that had endeared me to him in the first place back in our old school, but now…well, cute wasn't what I was looking for. Cute in the physical sense, maybe, but I wanted class and confidence and assertiveness. I wanted a guy who knew what he wanted, knew how to get it, someone like—

"So, Sasha," Taylor approached. "We still on for Friday?"

He stood tall with hands in pockets, chin raised.

Huh? What was he talking about? "Um…" I gulped.

"I'll ah, see you tomorrow," Jordan said, offering a small smile and an even smaller wave. I nodded and returned his smile, then he walked off.

Taylor's posture relaxed. Oh, he was just trying to get me out of the awkward conversation with Apoca—*Jordan*.

"Friday?" I asked.

"Well, since you mentioned it, sure, let's meet up." He grinned.

Sneaky. Sneaky, beautiful Taylor.

My cheeks warmed. "Okay. Where?"

"Fish and chips at the harbor? About an hour after school finishes? I have to do something else before then."

I'd rather have caviar and some sort of classy, bubbly beverage, but anyway. "Sure. I'll see you then." I smiled.

"It will be the highlight of my week." He smiled too. Then he took my phone from my grasp. "Let me check that your phone isn't damaged from the collision with the new guy who likes your hair."

"It's fine, it's—"

Oh. I realized what he was doing. He tapped at my phone then handed it back.

"Just in case you're running late on Friday. Text me. Or call. Whatever." He shrugged.

"I'll be on time," I said, a buzz fizzing up inside.

"I better get your number in case *I'm* running late, then. Not that I will, but…" He handed me his phone.

I put my number in, for a moment going blank and forgetting what it actually was, thanks to hormone brain.

"Enjoy your afternoon," Taylor said after I gave his

phone back, turning to walk away then turning back again. "The new guy was right, your hair *does* look good. But he needs some help with color descriptions. I wouldn't call it reddish purple, it's more like a sort of burgundy, you know? And crimson. A burgundy crimson with a hint of purple." He smiled and walked off, and I stood still for a moment, stroking a few strands of my hair as if in a daze.

Yes, I wanted someone who had confidence, who was assertive, who knew how to take action to get what they wanted. Someone like Taylor.

• • •

After going to the harbor after school, having wandered and pondered (no College Dude in sight so none of that growing fonder business, which didn't really matter anyway, as Taylor was currently winning the hormone battle in my mind), I went home and opened the laptop to my blog:

> *I don't like math, but I'm counting my blessings…*
>
> *Yes, I know it sounds cheesy and all that, but I'm going to do it. Count my blessings. Well, list them at least. In a journal, and on this blog. Though I might not share ALL of them on the blog—a girl's gotta have at least some privacy!*
>
> *Each day, or at least, most days, I'm going to write what I'm grateful for in my new Blessings Journal. Here's what it looks like:*

I inserted a photo of the journal Mom had given me with the empowered woman (complete with her inner warrior) on the front.

Maybe I should also get a fancy new pen to write with, but for now I'll just use my boring old blue ball-point pen that I use at school.

Okay, so here are the first of my blessings, or things I'm grateful for from today:

1. Receiving compliments on my hair (thank you guys!).

2. Getting a bit of help in English class so I didn't look like a complete idiot.

3. Having some time out near the water to think about my life and admire the scenery (geez I sound old!).

4.

I deleted number 4 and opened my journal, writing the first three in and then a private one:

4. Getting asked out by Taylor. Woohoo!

CHAPTER 6

"Hit me! C'mon, hit me like you mean it!"

I sighed. "Savvy, I'm not going to hit you."

"Oh, c'mon, just a punch. I promise I can block it. Riley taught me how. You won't hurt me." My youngest sister stood in our living room, couches pushed back against the wall, standing in a springy stance with fists on high alert and ready to defend herself.

"Oh, alright." I threw a punch. Though it was more like a 'get away from me, you flying insect' than an 'I'm going to hurt you' punch.

"Sasha, that was pathetic. Put some meat into it, girl. I want to be well-practiced by this time next week for my first Taekwondo class. Riley's teaching me some awesome moves with his private training. Isn't he the best?" She grinned in that 'I'm so in love' way, then returned to her 'ready to fight' expression.

"Oh, alright." I tensed my muscles and imagined my petite little sister was a badass criminal. Even though she was wearing a silver ring with a love heart on it, which didn't exactly give her a criminal look. I'm guessing it was a gift from her 'isn't he the best?' boyfriend. I locked eyes with her, making sure she *was* in fact ready to block my punch so I wouldn't hurt her. Her dark eyes glared at mine with fierce determination, that same look whenever she got a clear vision and felt compelled to act on the premonition. She was ready.

I jerked my fist forward a couple of times to test her, then on the third I threw a punch toward her face. Before it had even gotten halfway, her forearm connected with mine to block it and she grabbed my wrist hard and twisted it downward, then held up her other arm at right angles as though ready to block a second punch should I continue my attack. Which I didn't. Because I wasn't that fast a thinker.

"Ouch." I rubbed my wrist when she released it.

"Oh c'mon, that didn't hurt!"

"It did!"

"Wimp." She sniggered.

"I don't want to play anymore."

"Hey, didn't you say you wanted to do more exercise for your New Year's resolutions?" Savannah stood with hands on her hips.

I crossed my arms. "No." But hang on, I think I did. But only in my head. Was she getting into my head?

"Well that would be a good resolution, so why not be my practice dummy and get your exercise at the same time?"

"Ahem, dummy?" I cleared my throat and raised my eyebrows at her.

"Okay, my practice ninja."

"That's better." I thought about her suggestion. "On

one condition. You teach me some self defense so I don't have to be the bad guy all the time."

"Deal. Okay, now you try what we just did. I'm going to punch you, you ready?"

"No, wait! What do I do? I forgot what you did."

Savannah sighed. "You block my punch and grab my wrist and twist it like so." She repeated what she'd done but in slow motion.

"Righto, got it. *I think*. I'll grab yours. Go." I stood at the ready.

"I'll do it slowly first."

"What the hell are you girls talking about?" Tamara called from the kitchen with a giggle.

"Tamara, you have a dirty mind," I said. "Go, Savvy."

She moved her fist toward me and I held out my arm, grabbed her wrist, and twisted it downward.

"Not bad technique, but you need to be faster, otherwise you'd be knocked out by now."

"Give me a chance, it's going to take more than one or two practice goes."

"It didn't for me." She shrugged, and I laughed. My sister, the sporty guru who could do anything physical she put her mind to.

We did a few more punches and blocks, and on the fifth (or was it sixth?) attempt I was awesome, if I do say so myself. I wished Taylor had been there to see it. Sasha the kickass ninja. I raised my chin. "What's next? Something *really* cool. Teach me."

"Do you mind if your hair gets messed up?"

My initial reaction in my mind was 'yes,' but when I realized I would most likely not be seeing anyone of the opposite sex for the rest of the day I shook my head.

"Turn around," she said.

"Umm…" I tentatively turned my back to her. I felt her grab my hair and yank my head backwards. "Hey!" I instinctively brought both my hands to the back of my head where her hand was but then her arm came around my neck.

"And you're dead." She let me go. "This is why you need to learn the correct technique, otherwise you open yourself up to further attack and give the psycho an opportunity to take you down."

"Well excuse me for not knowing the correct technique. I thought you were going to tell me what to do first."

"I wanted you to see what would happen otherwise, first."

"So what do I do if someone grabs my hair, or my neck?"

We swapped positions and she showed me. When I put my arm around her neck from behind, she grabbed my forearm with both hands and dragged it down as she moved to the side. My body kind of arched forward which somehow forced my arm to straighten and release her neck. Then she pretend-elbowed me in the groin.

"Geez! That's just wrong," I said.

"Gotta hit 'em where it hurts, Sash," she said.

"Should I be worried?" Tamara called out again, the faint scent of herbs and spices simmering in what I assumed to be soup, filtering into my awareness.

"All good!" Savvy maneuvered my body around and I prepared to be grabbed from behind, imagining it was the creep responsible for my dad's death.

She grabbed my hair and as soon as I felt the first hint of her arm coming around my neck I grabbed her forearm before she could take hold. That was the key, she'd said.

Once you're in a headlock it's incredibly hard to get out of one. I pulled downward, stepped quickly to the side and pretended to hit her where it hurts.

"Holy cow, you did it!"

Huh. Cool.

"Again?"

I nodded and we repeated the movements a few more times. "And then, once you've extracted yourself from his grip, what are you going to do?"

"High-five myself and grin in victory?"

She shook her head. "You idiot. You run the hell away from him. Riley says the first thing you should always do if possible is run. Then if you're lucky you won't need these fancy moves."

"Can't I at least take a moment to soak up the accomplishment of my badass self? Maybe take a snapshot of my attacker as he writhes in pain on the ground then post it to Facebook?" I chuckled, sweat prickling the back of my neck after the impromptu exercise/self defense session.

"If you want to risk being grabbed again, sure. Go for it."

"Okay, so what if he comes for me again, lunges at me or something?"

"If he's in front of you, go for the kneecap. Hurts like hell."

"I punch his kneecap?"

She tipped her head back in a laugh. "No, you kick it. Hard. Try and dislodge it to the side."

"Eww!" I shuddered.

"You can have your gross-out episode after you've escaped your attacker. Now do it."

"You want me to kick your kneecap?"

"Pretend, please." Savvy came at me in slow motion and I raised my foot and connected my heel with her knee. She folded forward and grabbed it, falling to the ground with her mouth wide open in pretend pain.

I almost didn't notice the front door opening.

"You should forget Taekwondo and try acting, sis," I said.

"Oh, someone wants to be like their darling Momma, hey?" Mom entered the house along with a gush of cool air, fresh oxygen filling my lungs.

"Hi, Mom. Savvy was just practicing her acting skills, but she's got nothing on yours."

She eyed her youngest daughter on the floor. "You doing Shakespeare or something? His plays have a lot of angst. You look angsty."

"My knee is experiencing the angst," Savannah replied, getting up. Mom gave her a kiss on the forehead, and then me.

"Something for you, Sasha." Mom handed me a small parcel. It was encased in purple giftwrap, with a small card attached.

"Don't I get something too?" Savannah pouted.

"It's not from me, it was in the mailbox." Mom shrugged, then went into her bedroom.

I opened the card and read the handwritten words:

Sasha, thought you could use this.

An anonymous gift.

Excitement bubbled up in my belly, much the anticipation of an impending scent vision, wondering what would await me. I slid my finger under the paper and lifted out the gift. It was purple too. But a sort of *crimson* purple. Like my hair.

"Nice phone cover, who's it from?" Savannah grabbed the card and frowned.

I ran my hand over the padded fabric of the protective phone cover which had shiny purple ribbon crisscrossing over it, and where each bit of ribbon crossed another, a tiny diamante was studded into it. It gave it a quilted appearance. "Wow. Very nice." I got my phone and snapped the cover over it, locking it into place.

"Taylor?" Savannah asked.

"Probably." I smiled, remembering him checking if my phone was okay before putting his number into it. And he'd heard my address so if he'd remembered it then he knew where I lived.

"Must have waited 'til we'd all left this morning, then dropped it in," Savannah suggested.

Or was it from Jordan? He was the one who had bumped into me. It had to be one of those two, but my bet was on Taylor.

"You're meeting up with him tomorrow, right?"

"Uh-huh." I nodded. "Maybe our New Year's kiss wasn't meant to be a one-off thing."

"If he kisses you again tomorrow you should totally blog about it. Take mid-kiss selfies and everything, give all the juicy details," Savannah teased.

I threw a playful punch at her and she blocked it in a flash. "Shame you didn't learn self defense before you were kissed—I mean *attacked*—by Apoca-lips. I wonder what the Taekwondo protocol is for defending against apocalyptic kisses?"

"I'm guessing it doesn't involve falling backward and twisting one's ankle."

"Probably not. Unless you do something to make the kissing attacker fall backward and twist *his* ankle."

"What on earth are you guys talking about?" Tamara came out from the kitchen, apparently unaware she had a smudge of some green herb or something stuck to her cheek. I decided not to enlighten her, just for fun.

"Taekwondo. Apocalypses. Kissing. The usual." Savannah shrugged.

"Just another day for the Delta Girls," Tamara replied.

And a couple of hours later, after dinner, it could have been just another night for the Delta Girls. But when connecting with my sisters failed to produce any new clues on Dad's death, I became despondent. And angry. And frustrated. A kaleidoscope of emotions mixed and merged into jarring colors and shapes in my mind, but never with any degree of focus. Blurred, moving, dizzying emotions that made me feel unsteady and uncertain. Instead of chilling in front of the TV, I decided to try another resolution, well, *two* actually—watch less TV, and write poetry.

With my sisters in the living room and the bedroom to myself, I got out a scrap of paper and a pen. Maybe if I did end up getting the hang of it I could get another notebook to use just for poems.

I clicked the top of the pen and the scent of ink reminded me of school. Not the best inspiration for poetry writing. But then I wondered if Dad had smelled the ink as he wrote that letter to Mom, or was he completely overcome with the emotion of his words? Did his hand shake as he wrote? Did the paper crackle beneath his pen? What was going through his mind?

I tapped the paper, and then words came tumbling out...

> *Where did he go? Where is he now?*
> *We need to find the answers but don't know how*
> *What good is a vision if we are blind?*
> *What purpose is foresight if truth we can't find?*
> *Somewhere he lays, but where, where?*
> *Hidden away, I fear we'll never get there*
> *But fear can't win, it mustn't, it won't*
> *Somehow I'll persist, I'll...*

Damn it, what rhymes with won't?

I chewed the tip of the pen.

Won't, won't...

"Oh, screw you!" I scribbled over the page with harsh scrapes of the pen. I scrunched the paper up and shoved it under the mattress, then wiped a tear off my cheek with the heel of my hand.

It had started so well, but nope, I just couldn't do it. Couldn't complete it. How could I complete something when the only thing I wanted to complete was...incompletable?

Or maybe I was in denial. Maybe I *could* write a decent poem, but it was just too damn hard. Too emotionally confronting, like standing in front of a tsunami and letting it engulf you. It was too intense, too *real*, to give life to the words my heart was screaming to release.

CHAPTER 7

The only good thing about school was that it was a distraction. It was easier not to think about my challenges, or *feel* them, when I had to focus on such riveting topics as mathematical equations I'd never need in my whole life, poetry that was written by dead people billions of years ago, and the composition of stars and planets which I'd never get close to unless I wanted to become an astronaut. Why they couldn't teach classes at school like 'teenage relationships 101' and 'achieving your goals' and 'self defense ninja tactics' I had no idea. School would rock big time if they did, and I would be there every day, and maybe, just *maybe* I'd even sit right up in the front of the classroom.

The other good thing about school was Taylor. How any self-respecting female was expected to cope at an all-girls school was beyond me. Yay for co-ed.

When I exited the classroom where we had just learned about one of the aforementioned useless topics (I won't even bore myself further by specifying which one), I got out my phone. When Taylor came over to his locker and locked eyes with me, I dropped my phone on purpose. "Oops!" I picked it up. "Lucky I have this extra-protective cover!" I rotated the phone as though I was a TV model trying to sell the phone and make it look like the best thing ever.

A lopsided grin snuck onto Taylor's lips. "Yeah, lucky then."

"Yep, very lucky." I smiled widely and waited for him to ask if I liked it or something. But he just got some stuff from his locker and closed it.

"I'm going to shoot some hoops during lunch. See you later on." He winked and walked off.

Oh, okay. He doesn't want to feel embarrassed that he gave me a gift. How sweet.

"Do you like it?"

I turned to the voice behind me.

"I thought it would match your hair, and of course, protect your phone in case any other awkward, clumsy guys bump into you." Jordan also had a lopsided grin. What was up with that? Couldn't guys just smile symmetrically these days?

"Oh," I said, attempting a normal smile but in my surprise probably joining in on the whole asymmetrical fad. "You bought it for me?"

"Yeah. I thought you would have guessed."

"Kinda, yeah, I did, I guess." I put the phone in my pocket. Well, tried to, but with the padded cover it was difficult and I ended up looking like I had an intense itch on my hip or was desperate to go to the bathroom. "Well, thanks. I really like it. It was very generous of you."

"My pleasure." He pointed to the schoolyard. "Do you

want to go eat lunch outside?"

I opened my mouth to respond but someone grasped my arm. "Sash, come with me to watch Riley play basketball so I don't look like a pathetic doting girlfriend on the sidelines." Savannah tugged at my arm. I eyed Jordan with a 'sorry' expression. He gave a small wave and turned away.

When we got outside I told her the gift was from Jordan.

"Ooh, somebody still has the hots for you!" She nudged me.

"Nah, I think he still feels badly about the twisted ankle and also for making me drop my phone the other day."

"Guys only give you stuff if they want something or have the hots for you. Trust me."

"So you're the male species expert now, huh? I thought that was my area of expertise," I joked.

"I've learned a lot since being with Riley. The male species really is quite fascinating," she said in an old, scientific-type of voice.

Fascinating *and* nice to look at. I watched as Taylor warmed up on the court, bouncing the ball between his capable hands like he had complete control over it. And the world. And me.

"Oh crap, what if he thinks I'm here to watch him like *I'm* a pathetic doting girlfriend on the sidelines?" I suddenly became self-conscious.

"Relax, he'll probably love it. He'll put on a show for you. But he's up against Riley's team, so stand by for a battle of the boyfriends!"

"He's not really my boyfriend."

"Not yet. But after this afternoon at the harbor I bet he will be."

I gulped. Not a nervous gulp, but an excited gulp. An 'I-can't-wait-to-kiss-him-again' gulp. Geez, was I really that shallow that all I could think about was making out with him? Maybe I *should* spend more time thinking about the composition of stars and planets and dead poets and mathematical equations, just to balance everything out and avoid my brain turning into one giant hormone factory.

As the players moved back and forth, a new scent seemed to weave between them from across the court, delivering a sensory slam-dunk to my nose. I sniffed. "Are you using a new shampoo, Sav, with a kind of vanilla smell?" I asked. "Or some kind of hair product?"

"Me?" she said. "I'm Savannah, not Sasha. Don't get yourself confused, girl."

"It's just that I can smell something. It's nice, but it's kind of coming from nowhere. Well not nowhere, I feel like I want to look over there." I pointed.

Savannah followed my finger with her gaze. She gasped.

"What? What is it?"

Savvy's face went pale and she stared straight ahead, through the energetic boys on the court, as though they weren't even there. She shook her head. "It's nothing, it's…" She squinted, rubbed her eyes and peering forward. "Damn it, it's gone."

"What's gone, what did you see?"

She turned her head slowly to look at me, and whispered, "I think it was a ghost."

My heart pounded. "Dad? Was it Dad?"

She shook her head. "Sorry, no. A girl. Well, a young woman, she looked maybe a few years older than us. But it was just a flash, and then she was gone. I thought she might have been one of the students, but she looked out of place somehow."

I scanned the surroundings, and sniffed some more. The scent was gone. "So I'm guessing you didn't recognize her?"

"Nope."

"Oh well. Maybe she'll appear again sometime. I'll keep an eye out, I mean, a *nose* out, for the same vanilla smell."

"Guess that's all we can do, watch and wait." Savannah returned her gaze to the players and sent an encouraging wave to Riley. She seemed to be slightly more used to seeing those who had crossed over nowadays, especially after the encounter at the Jamesons' house before Christmas.

Our presence beside the court must have had some impact, because it was an intense game, and considering there was only so much time for lunch, they had to play hard and fast. Unfortunately for Riley (and his doting girlfriend), Taylor's team won. He slid a wink my way as he walked off the court, and I mouthed "congrats."

"I must have distracted Riley with my spellbinding presence," Savannah said. "I bet if I weren't there he would have won." She chuckled.

"Oh, please." I tipped my head back. "Get over yourself, girl."

"Hey, I bet you think that Taylor played better because you were there, am I right?"

I raised my eyebrows. "Um, isn't it obvious, *loser*?" I jabbed her in the arm.

"Hey, I'm not the loser!"

"Loser's doting girlfriend, then." I shrugged.

"Don't let Riley hear you say that." She cocked her head toward him as he walked our way.

"Say what?" he asked, ruffling his sweaty hair.

"Um, that it was a tough game but you played well?" I said.

"Hmm, something tells me you two were talking about something else." He made a show of rubbing his chin between his thumb and fingers, then shrugged. "Anyway, gotta go get cleaned up. Kiss first?" He leaned over to Savvy, who prepared her lips into kissing position and met his with a loud squelch.

"Gross," I muttered.

• • •

But there would be nothing gross about my impending kiss with Taylor. As I walked down the main street of town and toward the harbor later that afternoon, and after bumping into Serena and Damon as they exited their favorite café, I estimated (well, Serena did on my behalf) that I had approximately sixty to ninety minutes before I would be experiencing the time-stopping, mind-altering, body-tingling bliss of his kiss. First we would walk and talk, then share fish and chips, talk some more, then it would naturally progress to an expression of affection.

Serena's estimate was way off.

When I arrived at the pier to find Taylor standing there waiting for me, he removed his hands from his pockets and held them toward me. "Sasha." He smiled, placing his hands on my cheeks. "Like today's game, I've realized that if you want something you have to go for it. You have to forget about taking your time and you have to take action and annihilate the competition as fast as possible."

Was he likening our burgeoning relationship to a game of basketball?

"I like you. I want to be with you. I don't want to waste time dribbling the ball when I could just try for a slam dunk."

Yep, he was. I didn't know whether to be flattered or slightly offended.

He grinned his cute grin, and I was a goner. His grin relaxed and he parted his lips, bringing them toward mine.

Oh, hello there.

He kissed me warmly with satisfying, firm pressure, but as the mixture of seaside scents in the air swirled around me and blended with the taste of his lips, a new scent intensified, and I pulled away from him.

"What's wrong?" he asked.

"Have you been smoking?"

He dropped his hands from my face and feigned innocence.

"You have! I can smell it. And sorta taste it."

"Is that a problem?"

Compared to the New Year's Eve kiss, this was a definite step backward. And not just because it tasted weird, and with my heightened sense of smell was kind of overwhelming, but because I didn't want a boyfriend who smoked. It was disgusting.

But I wanted Taylor.

I was about to downplay it and shrug and say "oh well, as long as you don't do it around me, and brush your teeth before you kiss me again!" but then I remembered our old neighbor where we used to live who smoked like a chimney. Mom would spray her aromatherapy mists around the house whenever he dropped in to say hello and ask Serena for help with a crossword he was doing. Even then, before our gift appeared, the smell made me feel a bit sick. Like I was slowly suffocating. The guy died of lung cancer the day before his fiftieth birthday.

"Actually, yeah. It's kinda bad for you."

"So the packet tells me." He lifted it from his pocket. "But I only have a few a day, mostly all in one go. I'll just make sure I don't do it before I'm going to be hanging out with you."

He touched my arm but I flinched a little. Maybe I was overreacting, but the image of the empowered goddess on my journal flashed in my mind. This was my life, my body, and I didn't want to be exposed to second hand smoke or nicotine or whatever, and maybe if a guy really wanted me he would give up such a revolting habit.

I decided to test Taylor. How much did he *really* like me?

"I'll have fish and chips with you as planned," I said, my hands on my hips. "But I'll only go out with you again if you quit smoking."

Go me! All that self-defense practice must have given me a boost of self-confidence. Why settle for second best?

Taylor walked toward a garbage can with the packet. "Done. So, can we go out tomorrow?" he asked, his hand poised over the can.

"You're going to throw them out and quit just like that?" Wow. He must *really* like me.

Taylor eyed the packet. Was his hand slightly shaky? At first he looked like he was about to say "Yep" but then a tiny crease of trepidation lined the space between his eyes. "Well, I might need a few days to gradually cut down." He took a few ciggies from the packet, counted them, then tossed the rest in the trash. "That should do me. By this time next week I'll be one hundred percent a non-smoker." He gave a firm nod. "And in the meantime, I'll just have to make it up to you and win you over with my irresistible charm and wit." He flashed his cute smile and grasped my hand, bringing it to his mouth and pecking it gently with his lips like he was in some old-fashioned movie.

I turned my head to the side as it flushed, and tried to stop a smile creeping onto my lips.

"So, see you here same time, next week?" he asked. "I guarantee I'll smell only of sweat from my afternoon workout." He chuckled. "Kidding." He winked.

"Okay then," I said. "But…" I pointed my finger. "No kissing. If you're successful, I'll let you hold my hand and put your arm around me. And then if you're still a non-smoker another week later, I'll let you kiss me on the cheek. But only after the third week has passed will I let you kiss me for real." I gave him a teasing, testing smile.

"You're giving me a three week challenge?" he asked.

I nodded. "Are you up for it, Mr. Slam Dunk?"

He laughed, and a look of excited anticipation shone in his eyes. "I never turn down a challenge."

CHAPTER 8

Later that night, Tamara was over the moon that she got to have second helpings of dinner because I was too full from fish and chips, and Mom was over the moon that I boycotted television in favor of writing in my Blessings Journal and doing more with my blog.

I was over the moon that I had taken a stand to do what was right for myself, and not allow a gorgeous guy to get away with winning me over until I was sure that he was prepared to fight for me. Fight a mild addiction at least.

I shared a few blessings on my blog (receiving an unexpected gift, enjoying takeout by the harbor, and realizing that an epically awesome movie was coming out next month), then started to write about another of my resolutions...

Show Sasha The Money!

I confess, I've never seen that movie, the one with Tom Cruise, it's so ancient. But I do know the iconic line, and now my dear blog readers, it's time for me to talk cash. Yes,

I could do with some extra cash—couldn't we all? I'm not greedy, I just want to see if there's a way to make some money so I can ~~buy more stuff~~ donate to charity.

I giggled at my little snippet of humor, and hoped that I didn't really sound greedy, because although I would of course share the odd bit of extra cash with charity whenever possible, I honestly did just want to buy more stuff. Well, not *more* stuff, but stuff that I already bought, that Mom paid for. So really, I kind of would be helping out charity, it's just that the charity in question would be the Delcarta family budget. And anyway, what was wrong with spending one's hard-earned money? Okay, so maybe I'd forget about that other resolution idea to spend less, but hey—I was doing pretty well with my resolutions so far.

Apart from the poem…

I pushed the thoughts from my head; the two opposing thoughts that said 'actually, that poem was kinda good, you should give it another shot' and 'a poem is only good if it is complete, and you know you can't do it Sasha'.

I continued my blog post…

So, I guess I could look for an after school or weekend job, or I could try something entrepreneurial (is that a word?… Yes, it is! I just Googled it folks). So here are some options. Let me know in the comments what you think!

1. Casual work at a clothing store.

2. Delivering brochures and catalogues around the neighborhood (exercise, AND money!).

3. Selling my own products, like maybe I could learn to make jewelry or hand creams or something.

I shared the link to my blog post on Facebook and while

I was there I checked my notifications. A few minutes later a comment appeared on my blog from *modernprophet*:

Hello again! My third visit to your awesome blog! I think it's great that you want to earn some money. All those options sound good, but personally I think you'd be great at number three. Nothing beats being your own boss! ~ MP

Who was this guy?

I realized I hadn't checked the other comments from my previous blog post that had come in this evening, so I scrolled down.

Oh, modernprophet had left another comment, on my post about the Blessings Journal:

Good idea, Sasha! Looks like you're going to have a great year. As for me, I'm grateful to have found your scentsational blog ;) ~ MP

Hmm. This had come in half an hour ago. Now the third one.

Could it be…

Taylor? It had to be. Oh my God he was 'wooing' me. Sucking up to apologize for his smoking. But *modernprophet*? What exactly did that mean? Maybe it was some kind of reference to our English studies, but then wouldn't he call himself *modernpoet*? A prophet was supposed to somehow pass on insightful messages and predict the future weren't they? (In which case my sisters and I could be called modern prophets).

I replied to one comment with: *Why thank you, it sure is going to be a great year*, and the other with: *Thank you again, I do like the idea of being my own boss*. I almost wrote 'Taylor' but resisted. If he wanted to play a little game of secret messages then I would play along.

I approved a few more general comments, and then my

email pinged on my phone. I closed the laptop and swiped my phone. An email had come in from an address I didn't recognize containing a mixture of letters and numbers that didn't make sense. But when I opened the email and saw the signature, I knew who it was.

> *Dear Sasha,*
>
> *Great work on your blog. Saw your email address on the 'contact me' page and thought I'd drop you a note. I have a blog too and wondered if you'd like to look at it? (link in my signature). I don't share it with many people, it's kind of private. But I thought you might 'get it.' Let me know what you think.*
>
> *~ modernprophet*

I remembered that I had been about to read his blog when I'd seen his first comment and clicked on his username, but then my sisters and I had connected. I was about to click the link in the email when caution crept into my mind. Hang on, what if it wasn't Taylor? What if it was some spammer and he was sending me to a porn site or a link that would cause a catastrophic virus? His blog was called: Modern Prophet Musings. Sounded normal enough. I hoped.

Instead of clicking the email link I went to my browser history and refreshed the address I'd clicked before. Just a simple, neutral-colored blog theme with what looked like a decent number of posts. I clicked on About Me:

> *I'm just a regular guy, but this is my outlet for my hidden creative side. I like writing, drawing, and photography. But I don't think I'll make a career out of it, it's more of a hobby. I'm good with numbers too, so that's the direction I'm heading in, but this blog will be a way to explore another*

side of me. I chose the name modernprophet because when I write, I feel like I'm channeling something from somewhere, like ancient wisdom or some kind of insight that I hope some people might find interesting or helpful. It sounds a little crazy I know, so that's why I'm keeping my identity a secret. Happy reading. ~ MP.

Curiosity kept my eyes peeled, I clicked back to his posts and scrolled through to see what sorts of things he blogged about. There was a drawing of some kind of weird landscape, like a mixture of a garden and something supernatural or sci-fi. It was quite good. I scrolled further down.

Oh wow, he writes poetry.

I read one and my mouth gaped. He wrote damn good poetry. Better than I could ever hope to write. *Taylor, is this really you?*

I clicked reply to his email:

Hi MP,

Thanks for getting in touch. Can I ask…do I actually know you? I have a feeling I know who you are. I checked out your blog, your stuff is awesome. You shouldn't keep it a secret, you have a talent. Why not let people know?

~ Sasha

P.S – One of my upcoming resolutions is to try writing poetry, though I don't think I'm any good at it. But you've inspired me.

A few minutes later he replied:

Thanks, glad you liked it. And how do you know you're not any good at poetry unless you give it a good shot? Go for it. Feel free to run them by me for feedback before you post any online.

As for who I am…I could tell you, but then I'd have to kill you.

CHAPTER 9

The next day I wondered whether to text Taylor and just get him to admit that he was *modernprophet*, but decided to leave it. Although, it would have been good to get confirmation on my suspicion, especially as the last line of his email had made me feel slightly uncomfortable, even if he was just being sarcastic. But he hadn't even finished it off with a winking emoticon to indicate he was joking, and sometimes with the written word things looked more direct than they were intended to be.

I walked around the main street of town with Tamara who was helping me look for a job. I went into the nicest shops first. Gotta aim high. I figured if I could get something in one of them I would, but if not, I would look into 'being my own boss,' as *modernprophet* had said.

The nicest clothing store said they didn't have anything available, as did an accessory shop. A gift shop asked me if I had any experience, to which I said I only had experience buying stuff not selling it. But that was the same thing only in reverse, right? How hard could it be? Now the only options left were the newsstand and the fast food outlet. Urgh. The newsstand only wanted applicants who had finished school, and when I walked into the fast food outlet and was overwhelmed by the smell of rancid oil I knew I couldn't stand to work there without throwing up. Though Tamara was tempted to buy a snack.

An hour later I sighed. "Oh well, not meant to be. I could try those junk mail delivery services, but maybe I should just go ahead with making my own creams and stuff, yeah?"

"Give it a go, why not? It might take a bit of time and effort though."

"At least it will distract me."

"From what?"

I eyed my sister and without saying a word I knew she knew. The busier I kept the better. Less free time to ponder all that lay incomplete with Dad. I knew that was why she liked cooking so much too, apart from getting to eat the results. It kept her hands busy, her mind occupied, and probably also brought back happy memories of Dad when we were a complete family.

"Let's go home then and write down some ideas and figure out how to go about it."

"You're going to help me?"

"Sure. One day I might make my own food creations, it'll be good practice."

I slung an arm around her and gave her a squeeze, and we crossed the street. As we went to turn the corner, I glanced at the liquor store that was being rebuilt after fire had burned it to the ground last year. So much had happened since then.

I bumped into someone and stopped. "Oh, sorry!"

He smiled, and I looked up to meet the gaze of intense dark eyes. College Dude! What did I say to myself on New Year's Eve, that I'd probably bump into him again? Metaphorically, and literally. Maybe my psychic abilities weren't only restricted to smells.

"Hi." I smiled. He was even more good-looking in the daylight.

"Hi, ah…" He strung out the word and glanced upward as though retrieving a memory.

"Sasha," I confirmed.

"Sasha, that's right. You put the photo of the cupcake I gave you on Facebook."

I nodded.

"And we meet again," he said, looking at Tamara.

I had almost forgotten she had crossed paths with him at the harbor a few days ago when he had said to say hello to her 'cupcake loving friend.' Tamara hadn't corrected him to point out that we were sisters.

"Uh-huh," she replied. "Tamara." She held out her hand and he shook it.

It was then I realized he had never introduced himself, and he didn't seem like he was about to, so I prompted him.

"What did you say your name was?" I asked, as though he'd told us that night and I'd forgotten, which was a lie. Possible names flashed through my mind in an instant as I tried to practice my non-scent based psychic abilities. Or at the very least, good guessing skills.

Daniel…Sam…Dylan…he looked like he could be a Daniel, a Sam, or a Dylan. Or even a Jack.

"Alex."

Way off. Oh well, back to smelling the future I go.

"Nice to officially meet you." He held out his hand and I shook it. It was large and warm. Like he was wrapping my small hand in a thick, comforting blanket. Hands like that were protective, strong. As he released from the handshake I noticed the edge of a tattoo on the inside of his forearm, under where his shirtsleeve was rolled up at the elbow. I couldn't see what it was and was about to ask when he spoke.

"Are you sisters?" His gaze alternated between us.

"Yep. But wait, there's more." I chuckled.

His eyebrows rose. "Big family, huh?"

"There are five of us girls. Plus Mom."

"Sounds like fun. I only have one sister."

Just like Taylor. Guys with sisters often made better boyfriends, or so I'd heard. They understood the female mind better. Then again, Riley didn't have a sister and Savannah swore he was the Best Boyfriend Ever.

"Younger or older?" I asked.

"Older by two years, but she's always felt like a little sister to me. And my complete opposite; I'm tall and she's short, I'm dark-haired and she's blond. And..." His gaze went distant. "Anyway, I've just always felt like her big brother." He scratched his cheek then put his hands in his pockets, and I got the feeling there was something else going on under the surface. His eyes seemed to hold such depth, and there was a cautiousness, an on-guard presence about the way he stood. With Taylor, what you saw was what you got. With College—*Alex*—I couldn't help but feel I wanted to know more. He was the cliffhanger at the end of a book, and I wanted the sequel right away.

"Does she live in Iris Harbor?"

Tamara discreetly nudged me after I asked the question. I hoped I didn't sound nosy. Oh well, too late now.

Luckily, he didn't seem to mind. In fact, he removed his hands from his pockets and leaned one against the wall next to the shop on the corner that we stood outside of, as though preparing for a long, relaxed chat.

"Yeah, on the edge of town. She works from home, so she doesn't get out much; she's not the most social person."

"So I probably haven't bumped into her while not looking where I'm going around corners?" I smiled.

"Probably not. But I wish she'd get out more. Make friends. It's just her and her husband, but he works long hours." He did that distant gaze thing again. "That's why I'm here now before college goes back. Keep her company. And make sure she, um, make sure she's okay and all that."

Alex was very good at being intriguingly vague.

"Well, it's good she's got a brother to look out for her," said Tamara, and I got the feeling she was trying to wrap up the conversation and let this poor young man go about whatever business he was wanting to go about. But my feet were stuck to the spot. It was the same feeling I got when I watched reality TV, when you just knew someone was hiding a secret and you couldn't move until you found it out. Usually after a painfully long commercial break or even worse, on the following week's show.

"I wish I could be around for her more, but with college starting back soon, I worry." He glanced around, then he leaned in closer and caught my eye. "I just worry that something bad might happen to her."

His deep, unwavering voice sent a little jolt through me. Something bad? Like what? Tamara had given up trying to leave and was now leaning in closer too.

"What do you mean?"

Alex took a deep breath. "The thing is, her husband isn't the nicest man."

"Oh?"

"Sorry, I shouldn't be telling you about this." He waved his hand and looked away.

But I wanted to know more. "No, it's okay. You can trust us." I glanced at Tamara and she nodded. The guy looked seriously torn up inside.

"I think he's hitting her," he whispered. "In fact, I'm sure of it."

My jaw clenched.

"She stands up for him and won't admit to anything. So I'm hanging around as much as I can."

"That's awful," said Tamara.

"Bastard," I said. "Is there anything we can do to help?" Like possibly predict what may happen to her and how we can prevent it? How we can convince her to leave him?

"No, no. I don't want to draw anyone into it. I'm trying to figure out the best way to either confront him, or convince my sister to move on without making things worse. Or get some kind of domestic violence people to help. But I need her to admit to it first, she just denies it. And if he is hurting her, then she's probably scared he'll hurt her more if she leaves."

I felt torn up inside. How anyone could get away with something like that I had no idea. How a woman could put up with that I had no idea, but I guess leaving was easier said than done. Maybe our visions *could* somehow be of help, maybe that's why we crossed paths with Alex—not because he's potential boyfriend material (not anymore at least, not since Taylor and I started moving forward—so long as he keeps up his bargain to quit smoking), but because we were needed.

"Do you think it would help to go to the cops?" I asked.

Alex's face turned steely. "He *is* the cops."

"Her husband is a cop and he's hitting her?" Great. Who could be trusted? No wonder Alex was hesitant to take action, when the jerk could potentially mess things up for him as well. Could even turn it around and make it look like Alex was hitting his own sister. My fingers matched the clenching of my jaw.

"It's a tricky situation." Alex chewed his bottom lip. "Anyway, I better go. Please keep it to yourselves." He lightly touched my arm to assure I complied. I nodded. Except, it was possible I might tell my other sisters, only because it could have an impact on our visions. But I couldn't exactly tell him that.

Our visions…

My mind flashed back.

The rock. Weapon. Hit on the head.

Oh my God. What if his sister had something to do with the violence we'd sensed? What if she really was in danger, and somehow, someway, we were burdened with the task of helping Alex to stop it? Or, I thought, as I recalled what Savannah had said about the hand holding the rock possibly belonging to a female, stop his sister from making a huge mistake that, although it might save her from further violence, could put her in prison.

After saying goodbye, I was about to ask him how we could get in touch with him but I'd thought of it too late. He had already disappeared around the corner. But I knew that the way life and fate panned out for us these days, if we were meant to bump into each other again, I was sure we would.

As we walked off, I stopped suddenly and Tamara asked, "What is it?"

I struggled to contain my emotions; it was as though my insides had liquefied and become unstable. I could smell Dad's cologne.

CHAPTER 10

"Hit me!" I pointed to my face as I approached Savannah in the living room when Tamara and I arrived home. "I'm ready. C'mon!"

Savvy's eyebrows rose. "The thing is, most punches come when you're not ready for them. I'll have to pretend-hit you when you're least expecting it if you really want to become a kickass self defense ninja." She grinned.

"Well, for now, I just want to practice." My muscles were tense and I needed to let off steam, as on the walk home I pondered (word of the week) what Alex had said about his sister. No way would I ever let someone do that to me.

She came up and threw a punch. I blocked it and twisted her arm then stepped away. She came at me again. I pretend-kicked her kneecap. She pretend-wailed in pain. I turned away and she pretend-grabbed me around the neck. I pulled her arm down and pretend-elbowed her in the groin. And then, Serena dashed out of the kitchen in tears. Not pretend-tears, but real tears.

"It's okay, we're not really fighting," I said. She looked at me with red-rimmed, glossy eyes and then shook her head.

"Sweetheart, hang on." Mom dashed out of the kitchen too and followed Serena.

"What's wrong?" asked Savannah and I at the same time.

Tamara stood from the couch and Talia emerged from her bedroom.

"Oh great, an audience, just what I want!" Serena covered her eyes. "I'm going to lie down for a while and then go to Damon's." She went toward our room but Mom grasped her gently around the shoulders.

"Honey, let's talk." Mom glanced back at the rest of us. "All of you. Let's just sit down for a moment and talk it out. Let out all your concerns about your father and I'll confirm everything I know. Will that make you feel better?" She turned back to Serena, who shrugged.

"C'mon." Mom ushered us to sit on the couches. Her floral perfume wafted in the air and as though it was a hypnotic sedative, I relaxed onto the couch with my sisters, suddenly drained, but also curious. Was she going to tell us anything new about Dad? Or was it just one of those family chats to make sure everything was out in the open and everyone's feelings were being considered?

Talia held onto Serena's hand and rubbed it with her thumb. Tamara offered her the bowl of nuts that were on the coffee table, and Savannah looked Mom square in the eyes. "Is there anything else we should know about Dad?" Savannah asked.

Mom opened her mouth but closed it when a knock sounded at the door.

"I'll get it," I said, getting up. I opened the door expecting to see Mr. Jenkins asking to borrow something or dropping in some helpful item or book for Mom, or Riley here to see Savannah, but it was Riley's brother, Leo. Framed by the door, he stood tall and strong but his face was pale, and the shadows under his eyes matched the shadow-like hair of his closely shaven head and faint beard.

"Hi, Sasha," he said, then his gaze peered inside. "Riley here?"

"Nope," I replied.

Tamara stood. "Do you know where he is, Savvy?" she asked, clearly trying to look helpful in front of Leo.

"He's at the gym. Probably be back in about half an hour."

Leo nodded. "Thanks. Tried to call him but he wasn't answering his phone."

"He's probably in the middle of his fiftieth set of bench presses." Savvy chuckled.

"Probably." Leo looked like he did a few bench presses of his own, with his broad shoulders. Though maybe all that chopping and mixing and blending of food in the restaurant was a sufficient enough workout.

"Do you want to come in and wait for him?" asked Tamara. "He'll probably come straight here after, won't he Savvy?" Tamara's usual relaxed and 'whatever' demeanor morphed into an awkwardness that looked more like Serena had appeared when she first got friendly with Damon last year.

"No thanks. I had to leave work early—coming down with some kind of bug. I don't want to pass it on." At his own words he stepped back a little. So did I. Getting sick wasn't on my list of New Year's resolutions.

"Oh you poor thing." Mom stood too. "Anything I can do to help?"

"No, but thanks." He offered a weak smile.

"Well, if there is don't hesitate to let me know."

He nodded, turned, then turned back and looked at me. "Nice hair by the way."

"Um, thanks." I stroked my hair. The guy had barely spoken to us and now he was complimenting my hair?

I closed the door and Tamara closed her arms over her chest. "Why do you always get all the attention?"

"Huh?"

"You've got Taylor. And Apoca-lips, come to think of it. Oh and I bet Alex finds you attractive too. Isn't that enough?" She sat down and huffed.

"Who's Alex?" Savannah asked.

I opened my mouth but Mom spoke. "Hey now, don't overreact, sweetie. He was just complimenting her hair. It doesn't mean he likes her in that way."

"Doesn't mean he doesn't either."

That was true. Was it possible Leo really thought of me in that way?

"I think he's dating a girl from work anyway," Savannah said.

"What? You didn't tell me that!" Tamara stood again.

"Settle girl, I might be wrong. I just know he met up with someone recently. It could have just been a work thing." She shrugged. "And I'm sure if you were the one who'd died your hair purple—sorry, *burgundy crimson*—he would have complimented yours." She offered a reassuring smile.

"Yes. And I don't have any feelings for him, so there's nothing to worry about, 'kay?" I patted my sister on the arm.

"'Kay," she mumbled.

"Now, where were we?" I said.

Mom cleared her throat. "Right. Your father. Well, let's just make sure we're all on the same page." We settled into our seated positions and Mom fiddled with her wedding ring, which she had taken off her finger recently and hung from a necklace, to keep Dad always with her but also not look like she was a married woman. "Serena was a little upset because we were talking about the possibility of your father being involved with something that may have put him in danger."

"He wouldn't do that, I know it," Serena said.

"I agree." I smiled at my sister.

"You might be right, but I think we need to consider all possibilities if we're to have any chance of ever finding out what happened to him," Mom said.

Shouldn't she, more than anyone, be the one to defend his honor? I tensed and took a sharp breath.

"So," she exhaled, "I'm pretty sure you know all the basic details, but I'll go over them again. Your dad went to work one day as usual, though he was tired. He had two cups of coffee before he left, said he'd had trouble sleeping. I'd woken the night before at about two a.m. and he was still up, reading a book." Mom's eyes seemed to shrink within their sockets and her face seemed smaller, as though the memories were pulling her backward. "I kissed him goodbye as usual, nothing out of the ordinary, and he left. The last thing I remember of him is his back, slightly hunched from fatigue, walking out the door, and his voice calling out, 'I'll see you tonight.' But I never did." Mom's jaw tensed and she gulped. Serena sniffed. And I longed to smell his cologne again. I also wondered why I'd smelled it after seeing Alex in the street that day. "When he didn't come home and I couldn't reach him, I called around but no one knew where he was. I left you girls with a friend and I drove to his office. It was locked, but some lights were still on, like he'd left quickly. And of course you know that his computer was still on too, as the police found a half-written email on the screen about the vacation he was planning for us." Mom clamped her lips together.

A vacation. What would it be like to have a vacation? Our lives had been one long marathon since that fateful day. Mom had never wanted to leave the house in case he came home. Until Savannah's coma when she realized too much time had passed and we had to make a change, go somewhere new, start again.

"So they suspected foul play. He hadn't taken his stash of spare cash he kept at home, and his bank account hadn't been touched, so there was no reason to believe he'd done a runner. And I knew he hadn't, I just knew. We were happy. And the letter…" Mom gazed behind us toward the hallway that led to her bedroom, where the letter rested inside the tattered shoebox along with other souvenirs of her past. "That was more proof that he didn't leave us, and that something had put him in danger. But the cops couldn't figure it out. The leads turned up dead ends, and as the years went by their time was taken up with new cases. The details of Dad's mysterious disappearance was left in a file somewhere to gather dust." That did it. A tear escaped Mom's eye and she wiped it away. The room seemed empty of all smells, and muted in color, like my senses had dried up. "I wish I could tell them that you saw his ghost, Savvy, but I can't. There's no proof that he died, at least not in their eyes. If only they knew, maybe it would help reignite interest in the case, once they realized it was indeed a murder investigation."

I shuddered at the word murder. It wasn't something you wanted to associate with any member of your family, ever. It was wrong. It was awful, and terrible, and it just wasn't fair. I rubbed the back of my neck and my hand warmed against my hot skin.

"So there were no valid witnesses who saw him after he locked up the shop?" Serena asked.

"Just the woman who owned the clothing alterations business nearby. She saw him leave and head toward the parking lot. She assumed he was going on a break or leaving work early. And there was no CCTV footage of the parking lot back then."

"So all we know is that he appeared to have gone to his car?" Serena confirmed.

"Yes. But he never drove the car. It was still there when I went to the office that night looking for him. The police fingerprinted the car in case he'd used it, perhaps with a passenger, and returned it, but it was useless. So the theory is that he either walked off somewhere or met someone in the parking lot, and went with them or was taken, or something. That was all they had to go on. So of course they delved into his past, but the people he'd gotten involved with back then all had alibis, and he didn't appear to have any current enemies or dissatisfied customers, and the case turned cold pretty quickly."

How does a perfectly normal father and hard-working small businessman go missing in broad daylight in a public place? Living with those unanswered questions almost my whole life was like walking into a pitch black room and not knowing whether you were going to bump into something, fall over, or be grabbed by someone hiding in the dark. And not knowing if you'd ever see light again.

"So you think that maybe, just maybe, he'd gotten involved with something bad and didn't tell you about it, and keeping his tracks clean to protect himself from getting caught was the one thing that ended up preventing him being found?" Serena kept up her questioning. I thought she may even get out a pen and paper to write down all the facts, but she probably stored them all in her busy mind.

"Possibly," Mom said. "If he did he would have had a reason. Money was tight; the business was doing okay but we had a lot of expenses. Maybe he saw a way to earn a bit more and didn't think it was a big deal if it was for the greater good, I don't know. I don't know what to think anymore, I'm just trying to understand why he hasn't helped us to know what happened to him. Apart from the fact that spirits can find it difficult to process and express to us what happened if they've been through trauma."

"It's been over nine years, surely that's enough time to process what happened to him? Why won't he just tell us?" Talia piped up.

"Time doesn't mean the same thing where they are," Mom said. "To Dad, it probably still feels like yesterday that it all happened."

I slumped back on the couch. We may have a gift that allowed us to get in touch with the other side somehow, but we were still as clueless as we were before all of this as to getting any answers. At least Mom had now revealed everything she knew, so that we weren't in the dark. I understood she (and perhaps Dad) had been trying to protect us by not telling us absolutely everything, and despite the fact that I often thought it was better not to know all the details, I was starting to think it was best to just get it all out in the open so we at least knew what we were dealing with.

I breathed deeply, hoping for a glimpse of something, anything, to help me feel close to Dad again. But all I could smell was Mom's perfume. And the faint old smell of our house, which now that I knew who it used to belong to after the fires last year, made me wonder if it was remnants of alcohol and ash. Then a new smell took shape, like a wisp of smoke rising up and dancing in a slow, rhythmic haze. I often got images with my scents, as though my brain was trying to find a way to understand what I was smelling. And as the scent deepened, I knew why I was imagining it as smoke. I could smell cigarette smoke. And now it reminded me of Taylor. Was he about to turn up at our door? Sometimes I could smell things right before they happened, like rain. The same way Serena could hear an impending visitor's car before anyone else could. I glanced at Serena, and she was rubbing her ears. She did it so often nowadays I could never tell if it was just habit or if we were getting that enhanced sensory thingy. But Savannah's eyes were squinting, and I knew. As Mom talked her words faded into the background of the cigarette smell, and I stood.

"Sorry, Mom," said Savannah. "We're needed elsewhere."

"Huh, where?" She appeared disoriented by her memories.

Savannah wriggled her hands.

"Oh. Oh, right." Mom stood too, smoothing down her skirt. Her eyes held a hint of hope. "I'll wait in my room."

Did Dad want to get a message to us? Maybe he'd

seen, or heard, or sensed that we were all in turmoil about his...I wouldn't say the word. His...disappearance. Yes, disappearance still sounded better, I was used to it. I wasn't used to the other, brutal word and the finality of what it meant that was like a blow to the head. A sudden image of a rock flashed in my mind, like what I imagined Savannah must have seen in our vision.

We walked to the bedroom. We could connect anywhere, but we were used to our space, our sleeping quarters that doubled as a portal to another world, a world we didn't fully understand, as though we were tourists, or aliens, invading a new realm. Though, it was more like it was invading us.

Like puppets, resigned to succumbing to these paranormal demands, we immediately held out our hands and connected. A jolt signaled the start, but I was ready for it. It no longer startled me.

Now for the bubbles. It was as though I was being tickled from the inside out, though not in an uncomfortable, tickly way. More like a pleasant tickle, like a soft breeze ruffling the hair around my face, or that popping candy that tingled and fizzed on your tongue.

The cigarette smell intensified. I scrunched up my nose. And then a huge whiff of it leapt up my nose and I coughed. And it felt like I couldn't breathe for the overwhelming smell, like it was soaked in a cloth that was shoved in my mouth and was taking up all the room and air. Only I couldn't feel the sensation, but my mind formed ways of picturing or feeling the scent to help me experience it more fully. I also had a sense of another smell, a human smell, like someone's hot skin and sweat. This vision seriously sucked. Luckily, the smells subsided, drained away like they'd disappeared down the kitchen sink in a swirling spiral of yuck.

I opened my eyes.

"Oh thank God, I can breathe again," said Talia, clutching her chest.

"I even felt that," I said. "Well, not felt it, but the smell was so overwhelming that it was suffocating me."

"So that's what was happening," said Savannah.

"What did you see?"

"A hand. Over my mouth. Only I could only see a bit of it, like I was in the point of view of whoever was getting their mouth covered."

"Was it like a 'shush they might hear us,' or a 'don't scream or I'll hurt you' kinda thing?" I asked.

"Definitely the second one." Savannah shuddered. "Did it feel like that, Talia?"

She nodded.

"Great." I sighed. "I could smell cigarettes, like the person whose hand it was had been smoking."

"And I guess you can tell what I tasted," said Tamara.

"Yuck," I said, remembering my kiss with Taylor.

Was this vision about Taylor? But he was quitting. And anyway, lots of people smoked. Well maybe not lots, but quite a few.

"Serena, what did you hear?" asked Talia.

"I heard a sort of a scream. Not a full on scream, but as though the person, a female, was about to but something stopped her." Serena tugged her ears. "And a voice. A whisper." She shuddered too. "His voice sounded awful, menacing and…I can't think how else to describe it."

"But what did he say?"

"He said, 'scream and I'll be the last face you see.'"

"Oh my God. Who was it? Did you recognize who it was? If we know then we can stop this, whatever this is." Talia tensed up.

Serena shook her head. "Sorry, I just don't know."

"Try hard to remember, think. Have you heard it before?" Talia asked.

"Maybe, I don't know. It doesn't ring any bells." She sat on the bed and smoothed her ponytail over her shoulder. "And he wasn't speaking normally. His voice was hard, forced, thick. Like he meant business."

My first thought when Serena had mentioned a man's voice was it could be Dad. But he wouldn't sound like that—menacing and dangerous. And he wouldn't say such a thing. And the person with their mouth covered was female, so that wasn't Dad.

I swapped looks with Tamara, and something clicked. Could it be...

Tamara cleared her throat and licked her lips. "Um, I have an idea who it could be. Who both could be."

Talia's eyes widened, and Savannah ran a hand through her hair.

"Sasha and I bumped into someone today. Do you remember the guy from the cake stall on New Year's Eve?"

"Yeah, he was hot," said Savannah.

"Don't let Riley hear you say that," I said.

"No problem admiring beauty when you see it." She shrugged. "Hang on, do you mean you think it's *him*?"

I waved my hand. "No, no, not him," I said. "His sister. And her husband."

Tamara nodded.

"His sister and her husband?" said Savannah. "Doesn't

sound like a happy marriage to me."

"Exactly," I said. "Alex—that's his name—he told us about his sister who lives on the edge of town. We're supposed to keep it quiet, but her husband is a bit of a jerk. Alex thinks he's been hitting her."

"Oh my God," said Savannah. "And she hasn't left him?"

"It's not that easy, apparently. He thinks she's afraid that if she leaves he'll come after her. Plus, he's a cop, so everyone probably thinks the world of him."

Savannah shook her head. "Great. So it's up to us to stop him somehow? How the hell are we going to do that?"

"We don't know for sure if the two people are them."

"It makes sense," I said. "Maybe that's why we bumped into him."

"Is he a smoker?"

"Dunno. If I happen to see Alex again, maybe I can somehow find out, bring it up in conversation."

"Good idea. Do you have a way to get in touch with him?" asked Talia.

"Nope. And I don't know his last name, just Alex."

"Damn, you could have looked him up on Facebook."

"I still could, but I think there'll be a gazillion Alex's."

"Not if you refine the search to those in this part of the world. Maybe he'll show up, or maybe he'll have mutual friends with you or any of us. Worth a shot."

"Okay, I'll have a look."

"Hang on, there's something else," said Savannah. "I saw a word. Like it was on a screen, maybe a password?"

"Oh?" I asked. "What was it?"

She chuckled and did a little flirty dance. "Goddess OfLove."

Tamara laughed. "That sounds like something you'd choose, Sasha."

"Ha, it's not is it?" asked Savvy.

I shifted on the spot and grasped my arm awkwardly. "No, no of course not." I scoffed. "As if."

Why would they think that? Hmph. But more importantly, why would Savannah see a password, *my* private password that I used for many online accounts, in her vision?

CHAPTER 11

Later that night after no luck finding any Facebook profiles that appeared to be Alex's, I logged into my blog. I checked my comments. It was kind of cool to see people were enjoying reading my blog, though most were just my friends humoring me. Except one, well unless *modernprophet* was Taylor. There weren't any more comments from him, but when I checked my email there was a message:

Any luck finding a job? And by the way, I'm waiting for you to send me a poem. Hurry up! You can do it.

I replied:

Nope. Going to be an entrepreneur I think. Starting tomorrow. And geez, patience please! I can only do so many New Year's resolutions at once!

I wrote my Blessings for the day in my journal, and also on my blog. They were mostly inspired by hearing about Alex's poor sister.

1. That I have a good family.

2. That I have a roof over my head.

3. That I have a great future ahead of me.

I almost wrote: and that I have a secret interlude going on with some guy, but didn't exactly want to make that one public.

Then I shared my post on Facebook and included a photo of a heart with hands around it, like a way to represent that I was supported in all that I—*we* were going through. I liked to think they were Dad's hands.

I liked to think that somehow, he was indeed watching over me, and all of us, protecting us, making sure that we stayed safe and that someday, when we were ready, when he was ready, we would find out the truth and be released from this prison of uncertainty.

• • •

"Here we go." Mom plonked down a bag of stuff on the dining table that I was going to use to make my own hand creams and stuff. And hopefully make money from. I could already smell the essential oils and ingredients she had picked up from the day spa for me, and my senses tingled with anticipation. Sasha's Scentsations, I was going to call them. Luckily, Mom had spoken to her colleague, an aromatherapist, and she'd passed on some instruction sheets on how to make them. It was easy, apparently. Financial freedom here I come! And if it didn't work out, at least I would smell nice.

"I'm off to have a chai with Lucinda in town," Mom said. "Back in an hour or two. I look forward to seeing your creations when I return, my darling!" She kissed the top of my head and I smiled, then adjusted my hair.

Before I got started I posted on Facebook:

Sunday Funday—making my own scented body products! Watch this space. Sooo, what's everyone else doing?

Within a minute, Jordan commented:

Sounds like you'll have more fun than me, I'm stuck at a boring family gathering with hardly anyone under the age of fifty.

As I read through the instruction sheets, a few more likes and comments appeared on my post, including one from Taylor:

I'm walking home from a friend's house. In the fresh air. FRESH, I tell you.

I chuckled. He was trying to let me know that he was cutting back on the smoking.

Riley then commented, which was interesting as he didn't use Facebook that much:

Nothing fresh about where I am, just finished at the gym! And tell Savvy I have good news. Be there in a tic.

"Savvy, Riley says he has good news," I said.

She shot up from the floor where she'd been doing stomach crunches. "Ooh!" She checked her phone. "Then why hasn't he texted me?"

"He just replied to my post on Facebook, will be here soon."

She smiled, then walked down the hall. I heard the bathroom door bang lightly against the wall and caught a whiff of deodorant.

"Can't get any peace around here." Talia got up from the floor too, where she'd been meditating. Or trying to. She pulled on a sweater and opened the door to the patio, closing it behind her.

I opened the container of base cream, which was

supposedly fragrance-free. You were supposed to add oils and other ingredients, but to me it did have a smell. A smell-less smell, if that was even possible. Like a thick, hint of something, but not quite strong enough to determine. I scooped some into the small mixing bowl, then added a few drops of rose oil. Mom said it was expensive so not to use much, but it was so divine I wanted to tip the whole lot into the cream. I mixed it together with a small spatula, then squirted in vitamin E from capsules which I'd opened up. Everything had to be sterilized in boiling water before using, and thanks to my amazing mother, she'd done that for me before she'd left.

When I'd divided the mixture between a few jars, I sealed the lids and stuck a post-it on each as a temporary label until I made the proper ones. I smiled at my accomplishment. Rose-E cream, I was calling it. Mom (whose name was Rose) would like that. Too bad if there was something else on the market with the same name, this was *Sasha's* Rose-E cream, made with love. And a little bit of desire for cash.

My phone pinged with incoming email and I opened my inbox. My heart did a little flutter. *Modernprophet* had replied yet again:

> *If you won't send me a poem then here's one for you:*
> *Sasha is an entrepreneur*
> *The business of scent is for her*
> *She'll mix up creams*
> *To fulfill her dreams*
> *A more amazing girl there never were… I mean was.*
> *But that doesn't rhyme.*
> *~ MP*

My heart stopped fluttering and swelled with a delicious, happy fullness. No one had ever written me a poem before. I wanted to call Taylor and convince him to admit who he was, but no—I would let him crawl and suck up, make him stick to his challenge. This was going to be fun.

My smile remained as I scooped more base cream into the bowl, but instead of the thick, hint of a scent, I smelled a fresh, sweet, vanilla. *Huh?* I checked the jar to make sure I'd opened the correct one. Fragrance-free.

Déjà vu heightened my senses. Vanilla…I glanced around, it seemed to be stronger to my right, next to the patio door. "Savannah?" I called out feebly.

She emerged from the hallway. Something caught her attention and she gasped. "Holy crap! Scared the life outta me." She stood behind my chair and put her hands on my shoulders, to protect me or steady herself I wasn't sure.

Tamara came out of the kitchen, eyebrows raised.

"The girl?" I whispered.

"Uh-huh," Savvy whispered back. Then, "Who are you?"

I followed her gaze to the empty space near the door that clearly wasn't empty.

My hands shook and I put down the spatula.

The vanilla scent intensified; it didn't smell like food with vanilla, but had a definite soapy scent of shampoo or conditioner. "Does she happen to have nice hair?" I asked with a shaky voice.

"What?" Savannah whispered. "What's that got to do with anything? Anyway, shush!" She edged away from my chair and approached the 'empty' space, her hand slowly stretching out. "Who are you?" Then Savvy flinched and she turned sideways. "Where did she go?"

I could still smell the vanilla.

Talia opened the door. "What's going on? And why do I feel so tense? I'm supposed to be meditating and relaxing but it's doing the opposite right now." She rubbed her throat. "God, it's so tight. I can barely breathe."

"Yuck," said Tamara, who was wiping her mouth. "What's going on? I can taste blood."

"There's a girl, a young woman, but I can't see her anymore." Savannah spun around in circles like she was caught in a cyclone. "Damn it, where are you?" Then she stopped, and looked next to the fireplace-turned-bookcase. "Can you speak?"

We needed Serena, but she was out with Lara on one of their friend-dates. But then again, when ghosts were around, for some reason Savannah could hear them too.

The smell intensified, Talia clutched at her throat, and Tamara coughed, then it stopped. Talia sucked in a deep breath.

Savannah shuddered. "That was weird, it was like she couldn't talk, but wanted to. Her lips were clamped tight, and I heard a sound trying to escape, like she wanted to scream but couldn't." My sister looked at me and we both knew it must have something to do with the vision we'd had. The hand over the mouth. But that was supposed to be predicting the future, wasn't it? This was a ghost, not a vision, which meant that whoever this woman was, she'd already died.

I shot up, and my chair screeched. "What if we're too late? What if Alex's sister has been killed?" My heart raced and I ran a hand through my hair.

"Oh God." Savannah did the same. "Surely we would

have more notice than that, to try and prevent something?" She kicked the chair.

"Hang on," said Tamara. "Savvy, what color was the woman's hair?"

"Brown, why?"

Tamara sighed and her body relaxed. "It's not her. It's not Alex's sister. Remember, Sasha, he said she was his opposite and that she had blond hair?"

I exhaled in relief. "Oh you're right. Thank God for that."

"So who is she then?" asked Savannah, who had picked up a piece of paper and pencil and started sketching the girl she'd seen. It was pretty pathetic to be honest, but as long as it helped her remember the girl's appearance that's all that mattered.

A thought struck me. "What if Alex's sister's husband has been abusive to someone else before her? What if the woman is his ex, and he killed her?"

"Oh c'mon, really?" Talia asked. "It might not have anything to do with this Alex guy and his sister."

"Well, that's all I've got to go on," I defended. "Got any better ideas?" I put my hands on my hips. The room became silent. "Right, so unless anyone has a brain wave, we need to go with what we know. Somehow I need to find out from Alex if his brother in law had an ex, or if he knows if he has hurt anyone else before."

"Good idea," said Savvy. "If you can find Alex, that is. Otherwise, I have to hope that the ghost appears again and can somehow open her mouth to speak so she can tell us herself. We need to fill Serena in, in case she hears anything." She got out her phone and tapped in a text message.

I looked at my half-made creations on the dining table and suddenly lost all interest. I needed to get out of the house, into the 'fresh' air, and hope like hell that Alex was wandering around somewhere. How I could turn the conversation around to asking about his brother in law's relationship history though, I had no idea, but as usual, I'd figure something out when the time came.

I opened the door and gasped.

"Sorry, didn't realize I was that scary." Riley stood on the porch, slightly amused by my shock. "Everything okay?"

"Yeah. Savvy will fill you in." I stepped outside and told my sisters I'd be back later, and as I stepped off the porch I heard Riley say, "Guess who got a job behind the counter at the gym?"

At least *one* of us would be earning some money. Maybe I should keep looking for something else to do instead of making those creams. But then *modernprophet's* poem flashed in my mind: his humor and kind words and belief in me. And I suddenly I wanted to make *all* the creams, and read *all* the poems, and feel *all* the feelings because of a few simple words written just for me.

CHAPTER 12

As I walked around town with a hot chocolate in a cardboard cup in my hand, I felt like a private investigator. *Alex, Alex, wherefore art thou Alex*...See? Even when I tried poetry I just ended up plagiarizing Shakespeare. He was probably turning in his grave. Or thy grave, whatever.

I crossed the road and walked along the pathway that ascended toward Leo's restaurant. Though, it wasn't technically *his* restaurant, we just called it his because we didn't know the name of whoever owned the place. I walked past and peered inside, as discreetly as I could. Maybe Alex was having a meal, perhaps with his sister, taking her away from the house for a while.

I stopped for a moment as I caught sight of Leo through the gap between the counter and the kitchen. He wore a funny hat, and I bet Tamara would think he looked adorable. He moved about quickly, and I also had a sense that he liked to keep busy, to keep his mind off his Dad's death. I wondered if Riley would ever reveal to him the truth about their father. Leo needed to get some relief from the trauma. But, it all depended on whether he believed the fact that Savannah had seen his father's ghost. If Riley's initial response was anything to go by, it wouldn't go down well. Then again, if he knew that Riley now believed, now knew the truth, then maybe it would be easier to convince him.

Anyway, not my issue. Savannah and Riley needed to sort that one out. I looked back in front of me and started walking, but stopped again when someone rounded the corner in a run and it seemed like they were coming straight for me.

"Jordan."

"Oh, hi!" He slowed down, and although his skin was dark brown, his cheeks had a slight reddish flush to them.

"Everything okay?"

"Yeah, I was just going for a run. Exercising. Why, did I look weird? I bet I looked weird. Some people just shouldn't run, they look ridiculous. I'm one of them, aren't I?"

I tried not to giggle. He was so funny, in a cute, awkward way.

"You looked fine, I didn't know you ran, that's all."

"Started today. Which is probably why I looked weird."

"I thought you were stuck at some family gathering for the over fifties?" I asked.

He smiled. "I was. But I left early, told them I had some homework to do. Which wasn't a lie. I don't lie, just so you know. I just decided to go for a run first, get fit and all that." He put his hands to his hips and caught his breath. "Nice drink?"

I glanced at my cup. "Oh. Yeah. But it's pretty much finished now." I walked to a nearby trash can and chucked it in. "I might walk over to the harbor." That was the only place I hadn't looked for Alex.

"Oh, do you mind if I walk with you? I mean, jog, while you walk?"

"Sure, I wouldn't mind the company." *Just don't try to kiss me.*

"Cool." He began a slow jog alongside me as I walked across the road toward the harbor.

"So, do you like it here, in Iris Harbor?"

"I do now. I mean, I did at first too. But I'm glad there's someone here I know." His voice was wispy as it was carried on his strained breath from the jogging.

"It's always hard moving to a new place. Though with four sisters there was never any problem for me with not knowing anyone." I chuckled.

"Well, I do know my grandma," he said in between quick breaths. "And my aunt and uncle. That's why my parents wanted to move here, to be closer to family."

"Family's important."

"Yep." He nodded, though it looked like his whole body was nodding as he jogged up and down. "I should just walk, like you. I feel weird," he said, slowing down and walking normally.

I glanced at him and smiled. "Don't stop on my account. Jog if you want to jog."

"Nah, to be honest I'm wiped out. Phew! I don't know how anyone runs a marathon." He fanned his face. "Damn, now I'm probably all sweaty. And smelly. Do I smell?" He asked as he scrunched up his face. "Oh God, sorry, I'll be quiet now."

"Jordan, you don't smell, don't worry." All I could smell

was the salty air as it slid over the water, swishing and swirling around the harbor.

"Glad to know that high performance deodorant is worth the money then." He laughed. "So, um, last time I saw you, I mean, not *the* last time, but when we used to go to school together, you told me about your dad. Any developments in his disappearance?" he asked. "Sorry, I probably shouldn't have asked. I'm just curious. And I care. And I hope you're all doing okay."

The guy had no filter. His thoughts became words, end of story.

"Thanks. Um, no developments. Not really."

Except now I know that my father is dead. But I can't tell you that, because then I'd have to tell you that I can predict the future with my nose.

"Not really?"

Damn, should have been definite in saying no. "Well, no, but we did christen one of the bench seats on the coastal walk up near the cliff with Dad's initials. You know, since we don't have a grave for him."

He slid his hands into his pockets. "That's nice."

"Yeah, and it's right near the cemetery so it's kind of fitting."

"Oh, I think I know where you mean. I jogged past it. Great view up there."

I nodded.

"But there's still hope, right? I mean, he could still come back."

"Um…" As I tried to formulate a response the smell of the salty air became more intense. In fact, I could swear I could smell the different types of fish in the sea too, and the seaweed, and whatever else lived underwater. It wasn't overly appealing. My nose itched and I scratched it. But it continued.

Oh, I know what's going on…

"Um, sorry Jordan, I just remembered something I have to do." I gestured in the direction of the part of town where I lived. Where we both lived. "And you've inspired me."

"I have?" His eyebrows rose.

"Yeah, I might take up running too." I smiled. "I'll catch you later!" I waved, and just before I turned away I noticed him lift one of his armpits to his nose. I chuckled. Poor guy.

I jogged across the road, up the hill, and over to the coastal track alongside the ocean. I'd bet my life on the fact that my sisters were getting enhanced sensory perception too. The visions were calling.

• • •

"Okay, I'm here, peoples." I went inside and doubled over from all the jogging.

Serena was doing the same. "At least Lara knows our secret, she didn't mind at all that I had to cut our friend date short," my sister said. "In fact, she even ran back with me to keep me company."

Lara wasn't one of those people who shouldn't run. She was a running guru.

"Well, I'll be at home if anyone needs me," said Riley, waving and heading to the door.

"I'll always need you, baby!" Savvy called out, blowing him a kiss.

"Oh please. C'mon, let's do this." I led everyone to

our room.

We connected and when the jolt and bubbles had subsided, a nice, sweet, aroma filled my awareness. Like peaches, and strawberries, and some kind of green grass or plants, all combined into a new aroma as one. It was a bit like my Fresh Fruity Blast spray, but different. More specific, crisper, stronger. Then it faded and I could smell ink, and that scent of paper that was somehow so enticing, like book smell. But it didn't last long, because that awful cigarette smell overpowered it, and was then washed away by the moist, dense scent of rain. My nose was practically overdosing on sensory experience.

We dropped our hands from each other, and I filled them in on what I'd smelled. Tamara and Serena hadn't sensed much, but Talia was catching her breath. "I'm getting really sick of not being able to breathe properly," she said.

"And I really don't like seeing what I'm seeing," said Savannah. "Same thing as before, a hand over a mouth, but then the hand was on someone's neck."

"Like choking?" I asked and she nodded, then shuddered.

"I bet it's that cop. I hate him already. I wish we could figure out what to do about it."

"I'm sure life will lead us in the right direction," said Talia.

We were silent for a moment as Talia wrote things in our journal.

"You were in my vision," Savannah said to me. "I saw your nail polish so I knew they were your hands. And I recognized the edge of your bed. You threw something against the wall, I think it was a pen, like you got really angry all of a sudden and had to let off steam."

"Trouble in paradise?" Tamara suggested.

"Oh wonderful," I huffed. "I'll start meditating like Talia, shall I?"

"It wouldn't be a bad idea," Talia said. "For all of you, actually."

New Year's resolution number two thousand seventy-five perhaps?

"I'm home!" Mom called out as I smelled the aroma of fresh bread coming in through the front door with her. "Where are you all?"

Her footsteps click-clacked to the kitchen. Before she knew about our gift we would have had to pretend we were just having a sisterly discussion. It was so much easier now. In one way at least, the other side of the coin was that when she could tell we'd had a vision she'd try to act all normal, but it was obvious she was curious about what we'd sensed. Sometimes we'd tell her, sometimes we wouldn't.

Tonight we probably wouldn't.

After dinner, I blogged about other goals of mine like doing more exercise, and mentioned how I was being my sister's guinea pig for Taekwondo practice. I also mentioned I had taken up jogging. As of this afternoon anyway. I also posted some pictures of the jars and ingredients I was using to make my scented creams.

Lara Jameson, who had recently become a Facebook friend, commented on my blog post saying:

We should arrange a mutually convenient time to share a jogging session. I have some gaps in my schedule, contact me and let me know.

Oh God. Now I'd look even more ridiculous next to her. Maybe I could pretend I hurt my ankle again kissing someone, so I could get out of it.

Then Jordan commented. His first comment on my blog:

I'm honored that I inspired you to jog. I thought I may have turned you off it for life!

I giggled. Then I opened a Facebook chat window and typed:

Sorry I had to run off suddenly today. There's a lot going on at the moment.

He replied:

Hope everything is ok. And hope I didn't bring up any bad memories.

Me: *Nah, all good. Thanks for caring.*

Him: *No problem.*

I checked my email and remembered I needed to reply to *modernprophet*. Which was both exciting and daunting. Exciting because he wrote me a poem. A POEM. And daunting because I had to write him a poem. A POEM. But first I could just thank him for his one.

> *Dear MP,*
>
> *Thank you very much for your poem, it is both brilliantly written and perfectly true. ;) Kidding, sort of. But thanks. I'll do my best to write one, give me a minute. Or ten. Or a gazillion.*
>
> *Sasha.*

And then I started writing...

> *There is a mystery guy*
> *He's anonymous so must be shy*
> *He writes poetry*
> *And sends emails to me*
> *But who is this mystery guy?*

Not bad. Not great, but not bad. I sent it to him and bit my lip.

He replied back a few minutes later. This was like poetry on demand:

> *This guy shall remain a mystery*
> *Until in the future we've created history*
> *I'll keep emailing this nice young miss*
> *Maybe soon we'll have a moonlit kiss*
> *Now what the heck else rhymes with mystery?*

I burst out laughing.

"What so funny?" asked Savannah as she did her nightly exercise, lunging in front of me.

"Oh nothing much, just an email."

She peered at my screen.

"Hey! Privacy."

"Who's *modernprophet?*"

"Just Taylor. At least I'm pretty sure it's him. It's a username he uses online. He's been sending me poems and stuff!"

"Poems? He must really be trying to get in your good books."

"Well it's working." I smiled.

A moonlit kiss...ahhh, that would be nice. But only after he's completed his challenge. I typed a reply to my mystery guy:

Sistery? Kisstery? Zistery? I have no idea. But I like the second line of your poem, it's clever.

Him: *And what about the fourth line?*

Me: *Not bad either.*

Him: *So, whatcha doing right now? Apart from talking to me.*

SCENT

Me: *Watching my sister exercise. And another sister is meditating. And another is amusing herself on her phone with God knows what. I have a strange family.*

Him: *Meditating huh? Deep. I tried it a few times, I heard you're supposed to relax and breathe and go to your special place or something.*

Me: *In that case I would go to the cosmetics department of my favorite store.*

Him: *I would go somewhere overlooking the ocean. Do you like the ocean?*

Me: *Yep. Actually, I have another special place that overlooks the ocean.*

Him: *Do tell.*

I wondered how much to tell him. Taylor knew my dad wasn't around, but he didn't know all the details. I typed:

At my dad's bench seat, just near the cemetery overlooking the ocean. We engraved his initials on it to remember him by, since he disappeared we don't have anywhere else to go to honor him.

My chest became tight. And I felt like sitting there right now, under the stars, the salty air filling my lungs, a night breeze caressing my skin and tousling my hair.

Modernprophet replied:

I'm sorry about your dad. It's good you have a special place for him. Anytime you need to talk, I'm here.

I replied with a simple *thanks, that means a lot,* while inside my heart, I was preparing a special place for my mystery guy.

123

CHAPTER 13

Having finally created enough scented creams to sell over the next few days, I took photos and listed them on my blog, and shared photos and links on Facebook. I felt like a full-fledged business woman. Now I just had to remember not to use the creams myself. But I did make a couple for personal use. My favorite was Love Lotion. As I massaged it into my feet I imagined my future beloved giving me a foot massage after a hard day at work, whatever my work would be. Making more creams? Of course, I'd return the favor. But only if he'd had a shower first. Otherwise, eww!

I tapped my fingers on the keyboard impatiently. "C'mon, people. Buy my stuff!" I expected Serena to offer some kind of remark about being patient or allowing enough time for organic reach on Facebook to do its job, but she was in her own world in the corner of the living room floor, a large sheet of paper spread out in front of her. "What *are* you doing?" I asked. She'd gone straight there after getting home from her violin lesson. She'd even left her violin case by the front door, which she never did.

"Shh," she replied.

I stood and walked over to her, peering at the paper. She tried to cover it up but it was too large. "Is that one of those flow chart thingies?"

"Yes."

"Homework?"

"No."

"Fun?"

"No."

"Then why are you doing it?"

"Because I have to."

I moved her hands out of the way. My curiosity turned into regret. I didn't want to see this. "You're breaking down all the steps of Dad's disappearance into a flow chart?"

"What?" Talia gave up meditating and came over.

Serena's face flushed a little. "So what?"

"It's weird. And morbid. And…" I waved my hands about.

"It's helping me make sense of it all, okay? And maybe something will jump out at me, or any of us, and we can find another piece of the puzzle." She fiddled nervously with her pencil between two of her fingers.

"I guess that could be a good idea," said Talia.

"Well I don't want anything to do with this, thank you very much." I shook my head and walked away. A message pinged on Facebook, from Jordan:

Hey, so I just bought one of your creams. Not for me, for my mom. I showed her, hope you don't mind. I mean, not that I wouldn't use one of your creams if you thought it was good for me, or for a male, in general. But yeah, just ordered one for Mom. Thanks.

I replied to him saying thanks, and replied to a few more blog and Facebook comments, when Savannah came out of the kitchen and inspected Serena's flow chart. She scrunched up her face, not in disgust like I had, but in curiosity, then called for Mom to come into the living room.

"Mom, what did you say Dad had been wearing the day he disappeared?"

"Usual business attire, smart casual. Black pants and a gray shirt with faint blue pinstripes. Why?"

Savannah drew a deep breath. "I don't know if this is significant, and it's not something the police would know, because, well, they haven't seen his ghost, but…"

Okay, *now* I wanted something to do with all this, thank you very much.

"When I saw him last year, when we first found out he was no longer alive, he was wearing that outfit, but…" she took another breath, "he was also wearing something else, over the top. A kind of overshirt, or jacket of some kind. But it definitely didn't match his outfit. And it was kind of big, like it belonged to someone else."

"Describe it." Mom edged toward Savannah.

"Well, it's like I said, and it was kind of grayish-green like khaki, like some kind of protective gear or something a construction worker or factory worker might wear, I dunno. And I think it had a logo, or something sewn on the front pocket. But I can't remember it."

Mom's eyes went distant. "Hmm, he didn't own anything like that."

"And ghosts usually appear in the clothes they wore when they died, right?" Savannah asked, and Mom nodded.

"So this is like new evidence, except, only I've seen it."

Savannah rubbed her neck, then her eyes lit up. "If I get to see him again, I can look at it more closely. I can see what the logo is. Maybe then we'll be able to find out where he got it from, or who it belonged to!"

"And what if," Serena added, standing. "What if he did it on purpose, put it on when he knew he was in danger, so that if he was found, the jacket could link him to those responsible? Or contain fingerprints or hair or fibers or something."

Mom's eyes were wide now. "Oh my goodness, you could be right. Though of course, it won't mean anything to the cops unless…"

And I knew we were all thinking the same thing… find Dad's body, and we could potentially find out where he'd been before he died, and most importantly, who was responsible.

CHAPTER 14

"Sasha, another parcel for you!" Savannah called out louder than was necessary. She handed it to me. "Hand delivered in the mailbox. Another gift from Apoca-lips perhaps?"

I took the small parcel. "We shouldn't really call him that anymore."

"You made it up."

"Yeah, but I feel a bit guilty now that he's back in my life. I mean, not in *my* life, but in life, in general. You know what I mean."

"Oh, suuure, I think Taylor has himself a little competition," she taunted.

I ignored her and opened the package. Wrapped up in flowery gift paper was a small bottle of perfume. It was called Secret Garden. I hadn't heard of it—it must be just a cheap one—but the scent of it started to waft up to my nose even before opening the lid. "No note, so it could be from anyone." I was thinking Taylor, or his assumed alter ego, *modernprophet*. But since Jordan had given me a gift before, I knew it could just as well be him again.

"Give us a whiff," said Savvy.

"You mean you can't smell it yet?"

She shook her head. "But I can *see* it."

"Obviously. I can *see* it too. But I can already smell it."

"Show off." She whacked me on the arm.

I opened the lid and dabbed some on my wrists. Peaches, strawberries, and crisp green nature scents perfumed the air. With my sense of smell, this garden was definitely no secret. And then I grinned. "Ha! Prediction number one hundred forty-seven: true!"

"Have you really had that many predictions?" Riley asked.

"No, I was just making a point."

"That you girls are superheroes and I'm just the boring boy next door?" He chuckled.

"Yeah that," I joked. I rotated the bottle around, admiring its curvy shape that looked like a flower blooming. "Well, I like it. I'll have to thank my mystery gift giver tomorrow at school."

"What if they don't go to school?" said Riley.

"Hey, superhero, remember? I know what I'm talking about." I pointed to my chest and put on an overly confident voice.

Riley raised his hands silently in defeat. It was kind of nice having him around, he balanced out all the excessive estrogen and was beginning to feel like the brother we never had. At least, for me. Not for Savvy, that would just be weird. He also filled a tiny bit of that gap of not having a man around. Well, not having Dad around. And for Riley, he knew all too well what that was like.

• • •

For the whole next day I didn't mention anything to anyone about the perfume. I wanted to wait and see if Taylor or Jordan would say something. But I made a point of dabbing it on my pulse points at every opportunity to top up the scent.

At the end of the day, I approached Taylor at his locker. "Well hello there," I said.

"Hello yourself," he replied. "You smell nice."

Finally!

"Thanks. It's a new perfume." I gave him a suggestive smile, and as his wavy hair dangled deliciously beside his cheeks, his eyes looked at me with genuine pleasure.

"Whoever gave it to you must have good taste." He winked.

"Yes, they must." I smiled, and just by looking at him I knew I'd been right.

"Glad you like it. My sister got this whole pack of mini perfumes, and there were a couple she didn't want to keep since they weren't hot and spicy enough, or too fruity or something. So I thought I'd give one to you."

I chuckled. "Ha, thanks for the rejects." When his expression looked like he'd done something wrong, I added, "I'm kidding! I love the scent. I'm glad your sister didn't!"

"Phew!" He wiped his brow. "And guess what? No ciggies for two days now, none at all."

"Really?" I leaned in close to pretend I was checking for the smell.

"Hey, don't you trust me?"

"Of course, I was just joking around. That's awesome, well done. Keep it up."

"I will." He glanced around then leaned in close. "So, am I succeeding?"

"In what?" I whispered.

"In winning you over."

I wanted so much to say 'Oh my God yes, especially with that poem you wrote me', but resisted. I liked playing secret admirer.

I stroked the skin on his forearm lightly, as though my finger was a feather. "I believe you are."

His face brightened and he took hold of my finger. "So, maybe we should go to the harbor for fish and kisses. Oops, did I say kisses?" He whacked his forehead in an exaggerated way. "I meant fish and chips of course, but since I've said it, we might as well." He eyed me with his beautiful eyes that I could get lost in for hours.

I withdrew my finger from his grasp. "Uh-uh, Mr. Impatient." I wiggled my finger in front of his face. "Rules are rules. Today, you may simply hold my hand."

"And next Friday?"

"If you're lucky, you can kiss my cheek."

"And the next?"

"The next…if you're still smoke free, then I might… *might*…let you kiss me. For real."

Taylor tipped his head back with a frustrated sigh. "Argh, Sasha Delcarta, you are driving me crazy."

I just grinned and held out my hand. "Fish and chips await."

He glanced at my hand, then back at my eyes. He took my hand in his and we walked out of the school and toward the harbor, and I felt utterly, completely, in control of my life.

• • •

Later that night I lay on my bed and wrote in my Blessings Journal:

1. Taylor held my hand.

2. I received a gift.

3. I sold some creams.

And, I thought about the other day when Savannah had realized a clue related to what Dad's ghost was wearing.

4. Hope that there will be justice.

I closed the journal and held it to my chest. Like somehow the goodness it contained would filter through my body and heal my heart, boost it somehow, and bring more of the good stuff to my life.

I glanced over at Savannah, lying in her bed. She was talking quietly on the phone to Riley. "No, you hang up," she said. "No, you! I hung up last night." She giggled. Then she said, "But it's late! And it's cold out. And… Riley? Riley?" She took the phone away from her ear and held it in front of her. "Oh great, right when my nice pajamas are in the wash and I'm wearing my daggy emergency pajamas!"

"Oh wonderful," I said, covering myself with my blanket, as a tap sounded at the window next to Savannah's bed.

She pushed the drapes aside and wound the window open, and Riley popped his head inside. "Hey, gorgeous."

"Hi, yourself," I called across the room, then chuckled.

He smelled of fresh soap and manly deodorant or shampoo or something, and the room cooled as the night air whooshed inside.

"La-la-la-la," I sang with my hands covering my ears, as they made kissing sounds at the window.

I glanced at Serena to see if she was doing the same, but it was like she wasn't even aware of anything going on. She was lying on her stomach on her bed, her booklight propped up beside her, and with intense focus was writing on her flow chart. It was then that I realized that the missing pieces to Dad's death did exist somewhere out in the world. Just because we didn't know what they were didn't mean there wasn't a solution, a reason, waiting for us to find it. If only they would magically appear on the flow chart so we could retrace his steps and find him, and find the culprits. If only our Delta Girls magic wasn't the only magic we could do.

CHAPTER 15

My New Year's resolutions weren't going too badly if I did say so myself. I was barely even interested in reality TV anymore, since my reality was becoming more interesting. And I had even tried jogging yesterday with Lara, which I was quite proud of, even if I did lose my balance and fall face-first into a perfectly groomed shrub when we passed someone's house. And it didn't really matter that I needed two sodas afterward to replenish my energy levels while Lara only required a few sips of water. Yep, I would be a running pro in no time.

After being Savvy's guinea pig/punching bag in the morning, I bagged up my creams that I'd sold and walked around town delivering them to my local customers. *My* customers, how cool did that sound! Except now I had to keep making them to keep up with demand. I'd have to hire an assistant soon if business kept booming.

Serena left me on the street while she went to go meet Damon, and Savvy was at the gym where Riley was now working, apparently checking out the equipment but more likely checking out Riley. I downed a milkshake and scoped out some of the magazines at the newsstand, but like reality TV, I seemed to be losing interest in them. What I hadn't lost interest in, though, was the intriguing gaze of a young man standing behind the array of magazines and newspapers, flipping through one of them.

Alex.

Yes! I needed to probe further about his sister and see if I could find out how to help. And I didn't mind talking to him either. Of course Taylor was my number one, but that didn't mean I couldn't make a new friend.

He lowered the magazine and offered me a measured smile. Like he was pleased to see me but not extremely thrilled or anything. Not like the way Taylor often smiled when he saw me—a big wide grin that looked like it could split his face in half.

I gave a little wave. "Hi."

"Hi. How are you?" he said.

"Good."

"Good." He moved away from the magazines and newsstand, and I followed, like he didn't want anyone to hear whatever we were going to talk about.

"How are things with um, you know…" I asked.

He walked slowly along the sidewalk, I alongside him. "Let's cross over to the harbor."

Oh good, he definitely didn't want anyone to hear us. Which meant this would not be a conversation that revolved around small talk. Our visions needed us to get straight to the heart of a matter.

We crossed in silence, then with the water's slow and

rhythmic sounds as our background music, he started talking. "I'm thinking of just taking her away. Like, telling her we're going somewhere but then making her stay away from him."

"Like an intervention?"

"I guess so. Maybe with a bit of absence she'll see things how they really are and I'll be able to get through to her."

"Or it could do the opposite," I said, then regretted it. What did I know? He knew his sister and knew what would be best for her, not me.

He glanced at me with his intense eyes. "You could be right. I wouldn't want to get charged for kidnapping my own sister," he said with a small chuckle. "I just don't know what else to do at this point." He held up his hands and they fell to his side.

Now was the time. "Um, Alex? Was your sister's husband with anyone else before her? Like maybe he was the same with someone else, and they may be able to help get him in trouble?"

He thought for a moment before replying. "Well, he *was* with someone else, engaged. But it never got to the wedding stage, I think she left, or moved away, or something. Not sure."

Or perhaps she was killed and it was covered up.

"Did she have brown hair?"

Oops. How was I going to explain that question? I had just been thinking about the ghost Savannah had seen.

"Why do you ask?"

"Um, it's just that, um…you said your sister has blond hair right?" He nodded. "I read somewhere that abusive men often choose partners that look like their previous partner. So I just wondered, out of curiosity. Though I guess I should have asked if she had blond hair, oops!"

Alex eyed me curiously. "You're certainly thinking quite deeply about all of this."

"That's me, a deep thinker!" I said, patting my head. Big fat lie. When my thoughts got too deep I made them float back up to the top like a cork in water. Deep thoughts meant deep feelings, and although I was trying to embrace them a little more, what with my poetry writing goal and all that, I wasn't quite ready to receive deep thinker status just yet.

"I don't know what his ex looked like," he said.

Damn. But at least I now knew he had an engagement that got broken off or something. If he was this much of an ass with his current wife, it was highly likely he'd been that way before.

And then I had a thought (so much for not being a deep thinker)…what if the visions about the rock and the hand were not of the future, but of the past? What if we were seeing what he did to his ex, or someone else, and like our father, it was a missing persons case? Could the ghost be hanging around to try and get us to find her body? This was getting complicated. Although that theory was possible, I still had to presume that someone, someone alive, was in danger.

"Does he smoke?" I asked. "Her husband?"

Alex furrowed his brow to ask why.

"I also read that, um, abusive men are more likely to be smokers."

And clasp their hands over people's mouths and say: *scream and I'll be the last face you see…*

I resisted a shudder that wanted to rock my stability and send me falling into the water alongside the pier.

"You must read a lot. Yeah, he smokes."

Bingo. One strike for Mr. Jerk. Now, how the hell were we supposed to intervene? Maybe a future vision would give us the date and time and place where this attack on his sister would occur.

That would be handy, you know, Vision Master, if there is such an entity out there...hello? Anyone?

"Do you? Smoke?" I asked, but I didn't know why.

Alex seemed uncomfortable at my question; he slipped his hands into his pockets and his shoulders tensed. And I realized that there I was saying 'abusive men are usually smokers' and then asking him if he smoked. Nice one, Sash.

"No, it's an unhealthy habit," he replied.

"My thoughts exactly." I smiled, and even more so when the spicy, comforting scent of Dad's cologne overpowered the smell of the salty water. *Ahh, Dad. You're here.*

Then my smile turned into a frown when I caught sight of Taylor up near the boat ramp. He was smoking. "Um, sorry Alex, but I have to get going. Nice talking to you."

"No problem. Nice talking to you too."

I turned to walk toward my kinda sorta boyfriend who'd been either lying to me or had just given in to a moment of weakness, then glanced back at Alex. "Oh, hey, maybe we should keep in touch. Like Facebook or something?"

His eyebrows rose. "Ah, sure. But I'm not much of an internet person. Here, I'll give you my number." He patted his pockets.

I got out my phone. "Put it in here," I said, after pressing 'add contact.' He tapped in his number and handed my phone back, then I gave him mine.

I didn't know if I would ever call him, at least not yet,

but if anything further happened with our predictions and we needed to in order to help someone, then I would. But if that required me to reveal the Delta Girls secret, I had a strong feeling he wouldn't completely believe in our ability. But sometimes you had to do what was necessary for the greater good. And I hoped and hoped that someday soon I would get to write in my Blessings Journal something else I was grateful for: saving a life.

CHAPTER 16

"Two days without a smoke, huh?" I snarled as I marched toward Taylor, a couple of his friends moving aside for the oncoming inevitable Sasha attack.

"Oh crap. Sasha, it was just one, really." He stubbed the cigarette on the ground.

"Don't you have any self control?" I put my hands on my hips, and realized I sounded like my mother when she was having a bad day.

He gave a nod to his friends and they walked off, then he leaned in close to me and I stepped back at the smell. "I just lost focus for a second. Damn smoker friends. Peer pressure and all that."

"The Taylor I know would not succumb to peer pressure; you would more likely be the one *applying* the pressure," I said.

"Well, I *can* be quite influential," he joked, in a lighthearted tone.

I crossed my arms.

"Sorry, Sasha. That was my last one, I promise. No more." He made a crossing his heart motion with his finger.

"I'll believe it when I see it," I mumbled, turning my head to the side, the wind whipping my hair sharply across my face. "I better get home."

"Hey wait." He grasped my arm but I pulled it away from him. "Are we good?"

I shrugged. "I need to get home. I'll deal with this later." I eyed the hill that led to the coastal walk. "Actually, I'm going to go visit my dad."

"I thought your dad disappeared."

I turned back to face him. "He did. I'm going to his bench seat overlooking the ocean, near the cemetery."

Taylor's eyes asked for elaboration.

"We engraved his initials on it, so instead of a grave, we have a seat. My dad valued his life, Taylor, and you should do the same. No smoking, or it's not on." I turned and walked off. I didn't care if I sounded like a nagging old woman, he could take it or leave it. It wasn't just about the yuckiness of kissing someone with the added bonus of nicotine flavor. I just didn't have time for anyone who disrespected the gift of the life they were given.

And then I ran home.

• • •

The next night, after barely seeing Taylor all day at school, he messaged me on Facebook:

Sorry. I didn't smoke today, promise. And I won't tomorrow. Or the next day, or the next. I really want to be with you, and I'll do whatever is necessary.

I waited a while, thinking whether to reply, when he followed up his message with a photo, a selfie. He was pouting, his big round eyes pleading.

I have to admit, it did make me giggle a tiny bit.

The he wrote:

I'll stay looking like this until you reply. The fate of my smiling destiny is in your hands.

I made him wait a little longer, then replied:

I'll give you a second chance, but don't blow it.

The he sent another selfie, this time with a huge grin and his eyes so open and wide his forehead had horizontal creases in it.

You'll get wrinkles, I typed.

It will be worth it, he said.

And then he was the Best Taylor Ever over the next few days, and I enjoyed flirting with him between classes at school. Heck, even during classes at school when the teacher wasn't looking. I pointed to my cheek where I would let him kiss me that Friday, then he pointed to his cheek with an unsure expression, then to his lips with a 'yeah?' expression, but I shook my head. Amazing how much you could communicate without saying a word. And Jordan had helped me with another tricky question in class by using his itchy shoulder technique. Life was looking up again.

On Thursday, one day until my long awaited cheek kiss with Taylor, I stopped by Dad's seat again for a while before heading home. It seemed to bring me peace, even though any thought of Dad was always accompanied by sadness too. I silently asked him to help me, to help us. To come forward and give us some more clues. And to help us figure out how to stop this vague attack involving the rock.

When I got home, feeling drained, Savannah jumped up from the couch like she had an inbuilt spring. "Another gift for you! Quick, open it!" She handed me a rectangular box. This one hadn't been hand delivered—it had stamps on it—and the address label was written in capital letters, all fancy.

My energy lifted. Taylor was really going all out to impress me. I opened the box and withdrew a beautiful pen. It was black and silver with cute little circular shapes and colorful stars all over it. A small note was in the box, it wasn't signed, but said:

For your Blessings Journal.

I instantly felt all warm and gooey inside. I didn't know guys could be this thoughtful. I immediately took it to my room and placed it near my journal.

"I'm starting to get jealous," said Savannah as she came into the room.

"Jealous? You have Boyfriend of The Year, remember?" I nudged her.

"Ah, true." She plonked herself on her bed. "From Taylor?"

"Probably," I said. "I could get used to this!"

I posted on Facebook with a big smiley face emoticon: *Nothing like an unexpected gift in the mail.*

I also wrote a blog post and included the same, along with some other things I was grateful for in my Blessings Journal.

Savannah got off the phone with Riley and came over to have a closer look at the pen. Her brow furrowed slightly.

"What?" I asked.

"Nothing," she said, as though I imagined it. But whenever someone said 'nothing,' it always meant something.

CHAPTER 17

I sat at the dining table finishing the last of my breakfast on Friday, and finishing (well, trying to) an email discussion with *modernprophet*. We'd been talking about the injustice of teleportation not having been invented yet, not to mention the lack of trees that grew money.

"You coming?" asked one of my sisters. I didn't really know which one as I was so engrossed in the email I didn't register the tone of voice. "Don't want to be late for school."

Ah, it was Serena. Only Serena would worry about that. Or Tamara, but not because she wanted to get there and learn stuff, but because if she got a detention she would miss out on adequate lunch-eating opportunity.

"You go, I'll catch up." I waved them away.

Mom had already left for work, so I would have to lock up. But first, one more email to MP:

So, do you have anything to tell me?

I waited...

Okay. I have a question. Did you like the pen?

Aha! I knew it. He had to be Taylor and he had just given himself away by revealing he'd bought me the pen.

I LOVE the pen! It's perfect for my journal. Thank you.

He replied: *My pleasure. Maybe it will inspire some poetry too.*

Me: *And maybe I've inspired you to reveal your identity already! C'mon, I know who you are. In fact, I'm just going to pester you face to face until you crack.*

Him: *If you do that, I'll just deny it. I like our little discussions just the way they are. Why ruin the fun?*

Damn it, he was right. I didn't want to ruin the fun. I wanted the fun. And lots of it.

Just then a Facebook message popped up from Jordan:

Been meaning to tell you, my mom loves her hand cream, so thanks. I wonder if my hands feel dry. Maybe you can check?

He wrote the oddest things. It was like he wanted to do his absolute best with everything and everyone all the time. Maybe his contribution to my ankle injury had made him paranoid of making mistakes.

I replied:

Glad to hear! And sure, I'll shake your hand to check. By the way, shouldn't you be at school?

He replied:

I am, I'm just hanging around outside. What about you?

Me: *I'm still at home, running late. Guess I better go. Sigh.*

Him: *I'll wait 'til you get here and be late with you, in case you need company in detention. Also, I really want to know ASAP if my hands feel dry. I don't know how I'll get through the day without knowing. ;)*

I arrived at school just before the bell, and shook Jordan's hand. I gave him a three out of five on Sasha's

Scientific Dryness Scale (he made that up for me). Five was very soft, one was sandpaper. He was pleased enough to be a three, but decided I should make a masculine version of the hand cream that didn't smell like his mother's. I said that he'd probably be my only customer so I'd have to charge extra.

The day passed like any other, and when my mind had filled with more information than it could handle and I switched off my school brain (although, did I ever switch it on?), a happy feeling filled me up inside when I realized it was Friday. Taylor could take the next step in his challenge.

He came up to me at my locker. "Harbor?"

I twisted my lips to one side. "Oh, I don't know. Maybe I'll just go home and write with my new pen in my Blessings Journal instead, what do you think?"

"I think you'd be crazy to resist an invitation from such a handsome man as myself." He flitted his eyelashes.

"Aren't girls supposed to flit their eyelashes, not guys?" I giggled.

"Guess I got confused. How's this instead?" He tilted his head slightly to the side and flashed a serious yet curious expression, like he was some I'm-Hot-And-I-Know-It male model.

"Better. Now let's go." I slipped my hand in his. "But no cheek kiss until we get there."

He started running.

"Hang on, it's hard to run holding hands!" And also, while laughing. And also, just in general.

He slowed down. "Hmm, hold hands and get there more slowly, or not hold hands and get to kiss your cheek?" He rubbed his chin, which had a trace of stubble, not *on purpose* stubble like Alex had, but I'll-Take-What-I-Can-Get puberty stubble. "Race you there!" He ran again, and laughing and panting, I did my best to join in, my bag bouncing against my back as I ran.

We arrived on the side of the road near the harbor and he stopped. "Okay, close enough, now pucker up, buttercup."

"I don't think my cheek can pucker up."

"Damn, I was hoping you'd forget and just let me kiss you properly." He clicked his fingers in disappointment. Then he leaned toward me.

"Hang on, we're not technically at the harbor yet." I ran, okay, walk-jogged, over to the pier. "Now you can." I stood with my face angled to the side.

His soft lips planted themselves on my warm cheek. Once, twice, three times. "Ahh, now that was nice. See, if I'd let you kiss my lips you wouldn't have gotten to experience a simple pleasure such as that." I flashed a soft smile.

"I think a lip kiss would be a simple pleasure too. Why don't we pretend it's next week already, yeah?" He jiggled on the spot.

I clamped my lips down and inward, shaking my head.

"Argh, Sasha, you're killing me!" He looked up at the sky.

"Good things come to those who wait." I swiveled side to side in a flirty manner, grinning.

But my grin faded a little as I wondered if that was really true. Nine years, we'd been waiting for news on Dad. Nine freaking years, and all we had to go on was a strange jacket that Savannah had seen on our father's ghost. A ghost we weren't sure would ever grace us with his presence again.

"You okay?" asked Taylor.

"Yeah, why?" I brushed the hair from my face as the

breeze whipped it here, there, and everywhere.

"You just look a little pale. Like you've seen a ghost or something!" He patted my cheeks.

Oh, I wish, Taylor. I wish.

CHAPTER 18

I almost decided to surprise Taylor that weekend by dropping in unannounced, taking him outside, and planting a big wet one right on the smacker. But I was just feeling vulnerable and needy, as my emotions went up and down and shifted in and out of my awareness loosely like the variety of scents that invaded my perception. Only five days to go, and I would let him kiss me. Today, Mom had whisked us all off to a big shopping center out of town for a movie and some retail therapy. And as we sat at a café and ate banana bread and drank hot chocolate, Mom with her chai (though she'd asked if they happened to have any wine), I decided to get a bit of *modernprophet* therapy as he had sent an email earlier and I had yet to reply.

What's your favorite food? I asked, as I devoured the hot buttered banana bread.

He always replied right away, which I liked. He never kept me waiting. I thought he'd say fish and chips, but nope.

Cheese. I mean, who can resist cheese?

Me: *What type of cheese?*

Him: *ALL types. But the softer the better.*

Now I felt like eating a wedge of brie on a cracker. Instead, I took another bite of my banana bread, while Talia and Tamara debated whose slice of banana bread was the thickest, and Serena and Savannah debated whose boyfriend would win a quiz about their girlfriends. Mom simply ate and drank and watched the people passing by in the crowd. She said she quite enjoyed shopping centers now, whereas in the past when she was psychic, she would get bombarded with ghosts and end up having a panic attack and having to go hide in the restrooms. Savannah didn't seem to be affected by the same issue, unless she *was* seeing ghosts but she just thought they were regular people in the crowd.

I typed another email to mystery guy: *Maybe you should go into the cheese business.*

He said: *I wouldn't make much money. I'd eat all the cheese. ALL the cheese.*

Me: *You greedy thing.*

Him: *You started it.*

Then before I could reply he sent another email:

Seriously, I'm starting to wonder if I should head in a different direction in life. Maybe I could do creative writing, or study philosophy, or something. Do you ever feel like your life plan was just decided for you and you never got a say?

I thought for a moment. I did have choices, I was lucky with the life I had, but in a way, my life was the way it was because of what happened to Dad. Had he not disappeared, who knew if I'd be the same person I was now?

Sometimes, I wrote. *But I'm confident I can go in the direction I want. I think you should follow your instinct. What does it tell you?*

I finished my banana bread while I awaited his reply.

It tells me that you're the most helpful and interesting person I know. And it tells me I should do what I really want to do, even if others don't approve.

Me: *Then do it.*

Him: *I will. Thank you, Sasha. You're amazing.*

I got teary. Had I just helped someone with career and life advice? Maybe I should go into career counseling or life coaching. Then again maybe I needed career counseling or life coaching myself to help me stick to one freaking career idea at a time! Either way, I smiled. Life was full of possibilities, I just had to take opportunities when they arose and live life with no regrets.

"Does this slice taste a little off to you?" asked Tamara to Talia.

She took a bite and shook her head. "Tastes fine."

"Not to me. That's weird."

I took it from her and sniffed it. "Smells a bit weird though, mine didn't smell like that." It had a kind of old smell to it, and sort of a chemical aroma.

Savannah's gaze darted side to side. "Did this crowd just double in size? It seems very crowded."

Oh no, was she seeing a whole heap of ghosts like Mom used to? I shivered, wondering if ghosts were around us now and we didn't realize it. Maybe one was right next to me, stroking my hair. I shivered again.

Mom put her hand on Savannah's hand. "Just pick one thing and focus on it sweetie, it can stop the overwhelming feeling."

"Um, it's not just you two, I'm finding it hard to concentrate," said Serena. "Too many sounds."

I stood. "I'm guessing we need to, um…"

"How are we going to connect here?" asked Serena, pulling at her earlobes.

Mom stood, her chair scraping on the floor. "The restrooms. C'mon." She hustled us out of the café and we scurried down a corridor to the ladies bathrooms. But inside, one of the stalls was occupied, and two women were washing their hands. We stood about impatiently. I pretended to fix my hair and Savvy put lip balm on and Serena pretended to check her phone, until the two women left, and the one in the stall emerged and left too after washing her hands.

"Quick!" I said, holding out my hands.

"Hang on!" said Mom, dashing out to the door. She peered to the side where a storage cupboard was, and discreetly opened it. She pulled out a sign that said: *cleaning in progress, please return later.*

"Genius, Mom!" I laughed.

"I'll stand next to it and redirect traffic to the next closest restroom." She gave a nod, and I dashed back inside.

"Okay girls, we need to be quick."

We held hands and welcomed the bubbly sensation that rose and tingled from my toes to my head. It was like each bubble contained a different vision of the future, a different potential, and whichever ones popped when they reached the top were the ones we got to see. But although some of our predictions seemed random and inconsequential, there was obviously a grand plan behind it all. We saw, or sensed, what we needed to at any given time, not necessarily what we wanted.

I smelled cigarettes again, and sweat, and rain. And if blood had a smell then I could smell it. I didn't know how to describe it, just that whatever I was smelling made me think of blood. Which wasn't very nice. Then I could smell cleaning solution, like for a hospital.

When we disconnected I heard Mom telling someone there was a nasty mess in the bathroom and it would be in their best interest to go elsewhere for their toileting needs. I almost cracked up laughing, but was desperate to find out what my sisters had sensed.

"I heard glass breaking, but not really breaking, more like crunching. Like it was already broken but was getting stepped on or squashed," said Serena.

"Maybe that's why I smelled blood?" I said.

"At least you didn't taste it," said Tamara.

I scrunched up my face.

"I felt a lot of pressure in my head." Talia rubbed her scalp.

"I spy with my little eye, something beginning with R. Again," Savannah said.

"The rock?"

She nodded.

"It feels like it, whatever it is, is going to happen soon. Like we need to be aware. I hope we get another vision that's more specific."

"What else did you see, anything new?" I asked.

"Well, I did see the number twelve, but it was written as 12B. Like a sign, but not a house number, it was too big for that. It was painted on something. And there was broken glass. And a lot of darkness, except for some moonlight."

"Interesting," said Serena. We should jot this down. I'll put it into my notes app on my phone. In a flash she'd done it, and emailed it to each of us.

"Oh yeah, and I saw that GoddessOfLove password again," Savannah added. "Hey, what if it was that ghost's password and we need it to access something of hers to get evidence of some kind? Or maybe it's Alex's sister's password and it will end up being vital to enabling us to help her?"

"Yes, that could be it," said Talia.

I scratched my head and opened my mouth and was about to let go of my reservations and reveal the truth about it being mine, when a large, angry looking woman bustled into the restrooms. "Seriously, surely there's *one* available stall. For crying out loud! Oh look, they're all perfectly clean! Fancy that. Idiotic woman." She angled herself inside a stall and locked the door.

Mom dashed in. "Sorry!" she mouthed.

"Don't worry, we're done," I said.

"What is going on here?" said a voice outside, and as we went to exit the restrooms, a woman in a cleaner's uniform lifted the sign. "I didn't put this here. Who has been playing games with my equipment?"

Oops. I felt like I was at school, even though I wasn't the one who had put the sign there.

Mom put her hands on her hips and huffed. "Some woman did it, she told us we couldn't use the restrooms, but we managed to get in anyway. And they didn't even need cleaning! I mean, was she deluded or something?" She eyed each of us and we shrugged.

"Where is this woman?" asked the cleaner.

"She went into one of the stalls," Mom replied.

CHAPTER 19

"So, are you going to let him kiss you or what?" Savannah asked when we got out of the school library at the end of the day on Thursday.

"Who, Taylor?"

"Who else?" She cocked her head down the hall where he was walking along with a group of friends.

"Tomorrow, if he's still smoke free that is." I raised my chin.

"Well I hope it's better than the New Year's Eve one."

"That one was good, though."

"Yeah, so you said, but I hope it's even better. You know, raise the bar."

"Yeah, well at least I'll be prepared for it this time. And as long as I don't end up with a sprained ankle like the result of my kiss with Apoca-lips then I'll be happy."

"Um…"

"I mean, even without the ankle injury it was a disaster, and…"

"Um, Sasha?"

"Huh?" I turned around where my sister's eyes were urging me to look.

Crap. Jordan was standing right behind me.

"Is that what you *called* me?" he asked, and my heart lurched at the sight of his face. His innocent, vulnerable face that always looked kind and friendly now looked deeply disappointed.

"Jordan," I sighed, "it's not what it sounds like, it—"

"Don't bother," he said, waving me away. "I'll leave you alone from now on so I don't cause any more injuries."

"Wait, Jordan!"

But he'd already walked off.

"Nice one, sis."

"Gee thanks." I shook my head. "Oh man, how embarrassing."

"I think he's more embarrassed than you," Savvy said, one hand on her hip.

"Well, I'm humiliated."

"So's he."

"Okay then, I'm mortified."

"Again, he wins, Sash."

"Argh! Please, earth swallow me up now." I covered my eyes with my hand.

• • •

That afternoon Mom stepped in front of the TV when we were half-watching something. Well, I was half-watching, Tamara was engrossed as it was a cooking show. Mom grinned. "Ta-da! What do you think?"

"Mom, I'm trying to check out the height of that guy's awesome soufflé," said Tamara.

"Yeah, right, more like checking out something else," Savannah joked.

"Just because he's good looking doesn't mean I'm watching it for that."

"Tamara, I've been watching out of the corner of my eye and it's plain to see that his soufflé is nowhere near as good as the tubby hairy guy with the quadruple chin's soufflé."

"Hey, don't be mean! He can't help being tubby and hairy."

"Considering he openly said that his whole life revolves around food like that I think maybe he *could* help it, even just a little bit."

"Girls!" Mom shoved a coat hanger in front of us with an outfit hanging off it. "I said, what do you think? Of my costume for tomorrow night's work party?"

Luckily she'd told us beforehand that it was a costume party or I'd seriously be starting to get concerned about my mother's fashion sense, or lack thereof.

"Nice apron," Tamara said. "Now can I watch his soufflé?"

"Can I watch his butt?" giggled Savannah.

Mom moved a little to the side.

"Is the outfit from prehistoric times or something?" I asked.

"Ha-ha," Mom said. "Nineteenth century maid's uniform. And one of my colleagues is going as a Viking, he's going to look hilarious. Ooh I can't wait to let my hair down!" She jiggled then scurried off to her room.

"I thought maids had to wear their hair up," I said,

but nobody responded to me. So I opened Facebook on my phone, where people actually cared what I had to say. I typed:

So my mom's dressing up as a nineteenth century maid for a party Friday night, which got me thinking...if I had a costume party for my next birthday, what should I dress up as? Ideas anyone? Pictures?

I noticed Taylor was online, and so was Jordan. *Jordan... oh God, what have I done?* I clicked his name to open messenger and typed:

I'm so sorry, please forgive me. I didn't mean to hurt you, I was just being silly.

A moment later it showed that he had read the message. I waited for the little bubbly dots to dance on the screen underneath my message to indicate he was replying. But they didn't. Damn. He hated me. Or he could just be in the middle of something and unable to reply right away. I waited...*Nope, he hates me.*

Should I message Taylor and ask if we're meeting at the harbor tomorrow? Hmm...Nah, I'll just see him at school.

I sighed and checked my notifications, three comments on my post:

Dress up as one of your sisters. Easy!
A vampire for sure. With your hair it would look totally fab.
A nineteenth century maid.

I smiled, though I was thinking I'd probably dress up as a superhero. Then my email pinged with something from *modernprophet*:

Been thinking of you. I think we should meet up for real. Yeah?
My heart rate kicked up a notch. I smiled, and replied:
Finally! When? Where?
His reply:

How about at your father's bench seat, tomorrow?

I held a hand to my heart. How sweet. Taylor wanted to make our kiss extra special. I replied:

That would be lovely, kind sir. Time?

I waited a little longer for the next reply; he must have been checking his busy schedule, which probably wasn't busy but he wanted to pretend it was.

Sunset. I am going to take you out to dinner. Let's do this properly and make a night of it. Deal?

Me: *Deal.*

Oh wow, an actual proper date!

He replied after a few minutes: *Cool. *virtual handshake* I've made a reservation at Billie's, just outside of Iris Harbor, you know it?*

I vaguely recalled seeing it just off the highway before the exit ramp to Iris Harbor. Seemed okay. But I wouldn't know, we hardly ate out.

Sounds perfect. See you then.

"Hey, guys," I whispered, gesturing for my sisters to lean in close. "I'm meeting *modernprophet* tomorrow night."

"Who? Oh, that secret username for Taylor?" Savannah asked.

"Yeah, well I'm ninety-nine percent sure it's him! It's obvious, though, he wants to make a big deal of completing his three week non-smoking challenge and give me a kiss to remember." I fanned my face with my hands. "So, um, I'm not sure whether to tell Mom." I snuck a glance behind me to make sure she was still in her room. "She'll be out anyway, so maybe you could cover for me?"

"You should just tell her," Serena said. "She'd let you go out with Taylor."

"Yeah, but not if she knew that technically it was my secret admirer, and that I didn't have complete proof it was him. Even though it is."

"True," said Savannah. "Where are you meeting him?"

I told them the plans, and Savvy said, "Sounds okay to me, you can always just turn the other way if it's not him, or call us."

"Yeah, that's what I thought."

"I still don't like the idea of keeping it from Mom." Serena frowned.

"It's no big deal. Keep it quiet, promise?"

She sighed. "Okay, promise."

I took a nice deep breath and relaxed back. Tomorrow night was going to be a night to remember, I could feel it.

CHAPTER 20

The next day after school, I was anxious to get home and start getting ready for my mystery date. Tonight I would put my curl cream to good use and turn my super-straight locks into bouncy, sensuous curls. I'd also wear my new heels, my grayish/silver skinny pants that shimmered, and purple lycra long-sleeved top with the chiffon frills down the v-neck. Eating at a fancy restaurant required a little extra effort. I estimated I could look at least eighteen, if not nineteen, in that outfit. Especially once I did my makeup.

I went to head outside the school when I spotted Taylor. I grinned and decided to approach him. "So, ah, I don't think I can meet you at the harbor today. Maybe I'll catch you later on?" I smiled and twisted a strand of my hair.

He scratched his head. "Um, actually I have other plans tonight."

Oh yeah, OUR DATE! God he was funny, keeping this secret going on and on. I knew that when I saw him tonight he'd laugh and I'd laugh and we'd probably just get the kiss over and done with first up.

"I have to, um, help my parents with some, um, business stuff. But we can probably hook up tomorrow, yeah?" He raised his eyebrows and flashed his cute smile.

I smiled back. "Suuure. Tomorrow." I winked. "Can't wait." I held eye contact with him a moment longer then turned around.

Jordan was just about to walk outside. I rushed up to him. "Hey, I really am sorry," I said.

He continued outside and I followed.

"Hang on, can we talk? I think we should at least talk about it." I felt so bad about the whole thing and just wanted to get everything out in the open and dealt with, so that hopefully we could be friends again. He was a sweet guy, and I would forever regret his nickname if he never forgave me.

"I have to be somewhere soon. Maybe later." He shrugged and continued walking.

Here I was, chasing Jordan Davis, when it had always been the other way around. "I can't later, I'm going out," I replied.

Jordan stopped and turned to face me, his eyes holding a sense of curiosity but also...what was it? Dislike? Mockery? "Hot date or something?" he asked, and his gaze held steady with mine.

It was then that a bubble of uncertainty rose up inside me, then popped when it reached my mind. My mystery guy—*modernprophet*—it couldn't be *Jordan*, could it? I gulped. "Um, sort of, well, something that might resemble a sort of, um, date kind of thing." I tried to use my hands to speak for me, flitting them about like some kind of weird aquatic animal suffering from muscle spasms.

"See ya' later, Sasha." He lowered his gaze and turned away.

Oh no, did Taylor really have to help his parents with business stuff tonight and there I was getting all flirty and whatever with him, as though he knew what I was doing when in fact he may not? I suddenly felt unsure and strange, like maybe this date was a bad idea. Maybe I should email *modernprophet* and tell him the date was off unless he proved who he actually was.

• • •

I chickened out of emailing and decided to risk it. I could always run the other way if it *was* Jordan and he came at me in a fit of rage. Or I could simply use the date to finally talk to him properly and tell him again how sorry I was, and make the date a sort of apology, a 'make it up to him' kind of thing. But then what about Taylor? We were supposed to have our kiss tonight. I couldn't go out with Jordan if I was going to be Taylor's girlfriend. Oh hell, maybe I was overthinking things and my first instinct was right and it *was* him, and we'd go out as planned and then sometime on the weekend I'd find Jordan and make it up to him somehow, and then everything would be back to normal.

"Crap," I said out loud. *Modernprophet* I *did* have feelings for, whoever he was. But was that because we had gotten to know each other in such an interesting and intriguing way, or just because I thought he was Taylor? My head was about ready to explode.

I farewelled my sisters and reminded them not to tell Mom, and if she came rushing home having forgotten anything, to go turn the shower on quickly and tell her I was in there, or tell her I was across at Riley's house giving decorating advice or something.

It was a pain to walk up the gravelly road in my heels, but I tried my best to look dignified. It wasn't that far to the bench seat, and once I got on the pathway I'd be fine. As my shoes click-clacked much like my mother's did, I distracted myself by wondering where my life would be in five years, when I was twenty-one. Would I be the same old Sasha, or would I have morphed and grown into a different version of myself, a better version of myself? Would I be with the man of my dreams, or would there be years to go before I'd be lucky enough for that? Maybe Taylor and I would be one of those high school sweetheart couples who stayed together and everyone always thought the relationship was like a fairytale or a romance movie. I smiled. Either way, I knew that with my determination and assertiveness, I would achieve my dreams. All of them. I just hoped that when five years rolled around we would have all the answers about Dad, too. Actually, I hoped that we'd have all the answers well before five years' time—I didn't know how much more Not Knowing I could take.

Anyway, no need to think about that now…

I straightened my posture and prepared a soft smile, aware that I was approaching the hill and once I got to the top, I'd be able to see *modernprophet* from a distance, so long as he was at the seat before me.

But as I approached the top of the hill, I didn't need to see him to know who he was.

I stopped just shy of the top, as an overwhelming scent took all my oxygen and paralyzed my muscles.

Dad's cologne.

Oh my God. How could I have been so naïve? But how the hell?

I made myself move, slowly, up the hill, my mind going back in time and rapidly remembering every exchange with *modernprophet*, every feeling he made me feel. All this time, I'd been feeling these things thinking it was Taylor. It wasn't even Jordan. My vision took in the horizon as it grew in front of me when I reached the top. And there he was, his back to me, sitting on the bench seat, his dark hair matching his dark shirt.

He turned around and I gulped.

"Sasha, it's good to see you." He smiled.

I smiled an awkward smile, feeling exposed that I'd told him so much about myself. And yet, also kind of excited, as he still held a sense of intrigue for me, though after our online exchanges I knew a lot more about him now.

"Alex, hi." I tucked a clump of curls behind my ear. "It's you."

He held out his hands. "Surprise!"

I came up to him and he leaned in and gave me a gentle peck on the cheek. So much for my kiss with Taylor tonight, the poor guy *had* been telling the truth and was probably wondering why I was acting so strange this afternoon. Not to mention the other times I'd tried to drop hints and get him to admit who he was, when in reality he wasn't who I thought he was. And then I wondered if maybe he *had* noticed my odd behavior and been irritated by it and was just fobbing me off, not really wanting to be with me tonight. Oh God, I wanted to smack myself in the head for being so stupid!

"Sasha?"

"Oh, sorry. I was just processing it all, the surprise."

"You didn't know it was me?"

"Um, I thought it could be, but wasn't totally sure, I mean…" *Oh, Sasha you're a terrible liar.* "Actually, no, I had no idea!" Might as well be honest.

"Maybe I should quit college and go to acting school." He winked.

"Maybe," I replied, and his dark eyes drew me in the way they had done on New Year's Eve. "Though you could also be a professional poet."

He shrugged and smiled. "Maybe."

I couldn't actually believe that the guy I'd thought would think I was too young and not interesting enough was actually interested. In me. He'd allowed me to get to know him through the written word, while each time I saw him in town he knew that I didn't know it was him. I'd be hopeless at keeping a secret like that, I'd be all like 'okay, you got me! It's been me all along!' But Alex was clearly able to withstand such temptation. And maybe his online interludes with me were somehow a welcome distraction from what was going on with his sister.

I was about to ask about her when he asked me something. "So, have you been getting good use out of your pen?"

Oh yes, *modernprophet* had revealed that the gift was from him, but that only made me think that mystery guy was definitely Taylor, as he'd sent the previous gift.

"I have, thank you." I smiled and nodded. But then something didn't quite fit and a question mark formed in my mind. "Um, can I ask, how did you know where to send it?" I hadn't given him my address. Come to think of it, how did he even find my blog? We weren't Facebook friends, so maybe he'd just found it randomly in blogger land and recognized my photo.

"Oh, that. Yeah, sorry, I did a bit of detective work. Remember New Year's Eve you showed me your phone when you posted to Facebook? I saw your full name on the post. I looked up your profile and found you, and saw your link to your blog, and that's how I started communicating with you. I was going to friend you but decided it would be fun to do a bit of a secret admirer thing first." He lowered his face with a bashful smile.

"Oh, well, I'm flattered," I said, a bashful smile of my own appearing. But that didn't explain the address. I eyed him curiously.

"Oh yeah, the address. Well, I hope this doesn't make me sound desperate, but I really wanted to impress you and send you a gift, so I tried something out and luckily it worked."

I eyed him even more curiously.

"I saved your profile picture to my phone, the one with your new hair, and was able to use the location feature to see where the photo had been taken. I figured if I got the house number wrong one of your neighbors would have handed the gift over to you, since there aren't many houses in your street." He spoke like it was the most normal thing to do. Who needed the phone book? Though we weren't in it yet as we hadn't lived in town that long.

I nodded in understanding, but an uncomfortable wave rolled through me. First of all, I had no idea my location would be imprinted into my photos and that anyone with a smartphone could find it out, and second of all, though I was flattered that he was showing me how he felt about me, it seemed a teensy bit creepy. Like stalkerish. But as he'd said, he'd just wanted to impress me and keep the secret admirer thing going, so it was probably nothing. And anyway, he was a good guy who volunteered in cupcake charity stalls and looked out for his sister. He clearly wanted to be able to help people, and to be honest, he had impressed me. Those words of his, the emails, the excitement of it all. No guy had ever paid me that much attention in such an interesting and unique way. He had hooked me, and I was still hanging.

Anyway, it was all out in the open now, and we could go on our date and talk like we talked in our emails. Who knew what would happen to our online exchanges after this though. I could stop calling him *modernprophet*, though I didn't know if I wanted to stop. I liked the secrecy, it gave me a thrill.

"Well, I guess we should get going. A gourmet dinner awaits!" He held out his arm and I took hold of his elbow. "Oh, almost forgot. Change of plans, I managed to get a last minute reservation at a better restaurant, Valley View, at Fern Ridge."

"Oh, okay then." I nodded.

Then his phone beeped. "Excuse me, Sasha." He looked at it and said, "Sorry, I'll just make a quick call to my sister, make sure everything's okay."

Please let everything be okay. We still weren't any closer to figuring out how to stop this thing, and although Alex had revealed the truth about his identity and how he found me, I wasn't exactly ready to tell him the secret of the Delta Girls.

"Hey," he said into the phone. "Everything okay?…Well that's good then, maybe go to bed early, so you're not awake when he gets back....No, stop defending him. I know what he's like, no, you need to—" His face creased with concern. "Okay, okay, don't stress. But you can't go on pretending forever, something's gotta give....Alright, sounds like a plan. It'll be okay. Text me if any probs. Okay? Okay. Bye." He hung up.

Wow, looked like us Delta Girls weren't the only ones feeling the weight on our shoulders. The poor guy needed a break as much as his sister.

"Sorry," he said. "It should be okay now. I hope. C'mon, let's go enjoy our night." His expression of concern morphed into a smile.

We walked to the parking area near the cemetery, and he led me to his car—a glossy black pickup truck. It looked like one I had seen around, but then again, he wasn't the only owner of such a car. As he opened the door for me, my eye caught sight of slight movement nearby. I glanced toward a large tree, just in time to see Jordan standing behind it before he tried to hide. I furrowed my brow as I looked at him, and our eyes connected briefly. His brow was furrowed too. I diverted my gaze and hopped into Alex's truck. What was Jordan doing, spying on me? How did he know I would be up here...or maybe he saw me leave Roach Place and followed me? Geez, I now had stalkers on the mind.

As I did up my seat belt I felt a flash of guilt at going on a date with Alex when I was kinda sorta Taylor's girlfriend, or at least getting to be. But if he found out, or I just straight out told him, I'd say it was because I thought it was him, which was the truth. I thought about texting my sisters to tell them the identity of my secret admirer but didn't want to look like an idiot, so I kept my phone in my back pocket as Alex started the engine.

The sun was almost gone as we rounded the corner of the parking area and drove down the driveway of the cemetery, partly because night was just about here and partly because gray clouds muted the remnants of its glow. I hoped it wouldn't rain until we were inside the restaurant, otherwise my hair would go frizzy.

Alex turned the volume up slightly on the radio, and a cruisy song played. His car smelled new, like it had been cleaned well, yet it held a warm, masculine scent that was new to me. It was like being here with him I was somehow being initiated into a better, more mature phase of my life, in the company of an older man. I remembered Dad's cologne, which had since disappeared after I'd arrived at the top of the hill to meet Alex, and I did wonder if it was a sign of his reassurance, his approval, that it was okay to go out with Alex, and that maybe I shouldn't be putting all my focus on Taylor right now.

Alex tapped his fingers on the steering wheel as he drove, looking over at me occasionally as we exchanged small talk. "So, have you been to this restaurant before?" I asked.

"A few times. It's one of the best, and definitely the best in Fern Ridge. There aren't exactly many in the area."

"Right. Uh-huh." I nodded like I knew what he was talking about. I didn't know anything about restaurants and which were the best and how many there were in Fern Ridge. With Mom and Tamara being good cooks we hardly ate out, and anyway it was expensive. But I wouldn't have to worry about that tonight, Alex said he would pay for me. He told me he'd booked the best table, near the fireplace and a window overlooking the valley below. If this was what life was like for the girlfriend of an accomplished, intelligent, and generous college guy, then I could get used to it.

My mind flashed back to Jordan for some reason, the look on his face as he stood behind the tree watching me. It was a shame that our reignited friendship had turned sour. I'd tried to apologize, and I really wanted things to be back to normal with him, but it seemed like he wanted to hold a grudge a bit longer. Lucky he didn't drive yet or I wouldn't be surprised if he had followed Alex's truck. An ominous feeling made me turn my head to look behind us. There was a car further back—it was yellow. The color irritated me for some reason, and I turned back to face the front.

"Everything okay?" Alex asked, turning down the volume a little on the radio.

I flashed a smile. "Of course."

Silently he smiled. After a minute, he said, "Does it feel strange, talking to me like this, without the barrier of our online personas?"

I crossed one leg over the other, my ankle facing him as my high heel-encased foot dangled elegantly in the air. "Um, not strange, just…different I guess. But knowing who you are now, it makes it kind of…nice, too. We've had such great conversations." Why did I feel like I had to compliment him and boost his ego? Here he was, taking me out to dinner, and yet I still felt I had something to prove.

"We have indeed. And my poetry has gotten better because of you." He gave my hand a gentle pat. "You're kind of my muse now."

I could feel my cheeks becoming warm, and I fluffed my fake curls around my face to hide it. "Oh, I think you were already a good poet."

"A good poet is not enough…if you're going to be something, you have to be great, *more* than great, you have to commit to it one hundred percent."

Wow, this guy had determination. He knew what he wanted and went for it, including working hard to impress me. So what if his methods were a little out of the ordinary? My life wasn't exactly ordinary.

"So why don't you try to get some of your work published, get your name out there? I mean, your real name?"

He chuckled. In a way that made it sound like my suggestion was silly.

"A great poet does not need fame to achieve accomplishment, the achievement is in the creation of the poem itself."

"That's very humble of you."

He shrugged. "Besides, my anonymity has its advantages. It helped me get to know you, didn't it?"

He was right, although I would have gotten to know him the normal face-to-face way, or even online as Facebook friends. The secrecy about his identity had kept me hooked, wanting to communicate more and more, to keep the façade going. But the façade was no more, just like the façade of hope at Dad's disappearance turning out to be solved and him coming back—alive—into our lives, was no more. Reality had a way of creeping up on you, sometimes slowly, sometimes suddenly like the slap of a hand across the face.

But reality could wait until tomorrow. Tonight I was going to live the high life and enjoy every moment.

As we drove around the windy road, up into the hills toward Fern Ridge, the sunlight seemed to collapse in on itself behind the trees. Darkness rose and claimed the sky, and my nose tingled as the air smelled of fireplaces and coal, and crisp leaves coated with a hint of moisture, like they had already been rained on before the rain had appeared. I seemed to be able to pick up on these things automatically, each scent downloading a thousand different explanations for the variety of aromas, like I was one big scent-analyzing factory. The more I *scentsed*, the more I sensed.

Just as I thought, tiny sprinkles of water began speckling the windscreen. Not enough to obscure our vision, but Alex put the wipers on slow anyway. He slowed down, and the smell of fuel grew stronger. I jumped as the yellow car sped past, overtaking us.

"Idiot," Alex said. "One of the rules for good driving is to adjust your speed for environmental changes. Rain and roads don't mix."

I was glad I was his passenger and not the driver of the yellow car's passenger.

"I'll have to remember that when I learn to drive," I said.

Alex chuckled. "I keep forgetting you're only sixteen. In our emails, I always feel like you're the same age as me."

"I'll take that as a compliment. Just don't say that when I'm nearing forty." I chuckled myself. Then I cringed. Why was I talking like we'd be hooking up and embarking on a long-term relationship? Who knew where I'd be when I was almost forty? Sometimes I wished my voice was like a Facebook status I could edit or delete.

But he didn't seem concerned or scared off. He only looked at me for a moment, in a way that made me feel special. Older. Noticed. He looked at me a moment longer than was comfortable and I was about to remind him to watch the road when he turned his gaze back to the front.

"If I could, I wouldn't take my eyes off you."

Gulp. He sure didn't like to waste time. For some reason, somehow, he had feelings for me, and even though I had developed feelings for *modernprophet*, and I liked the real life Alex, I still needed time to process it all and merge the two together to see how they fit, to see how it all felt. Having thought I was going out with Taylor, my mind was still a bit confused and surprised.

"Don't be embarrassed," he said, and I brought my palm to my hot cheeks.

"I'm flattered is all."

"I'm flattered that you're flattered," he replied.

He drove in silence for a moment. The hill flattened out and the windy road tapered to straight as we neared the town before Fern Ridge, mostly filled with industrial properties. Alex checked his rearview mirror, then slowed even more, veering off and onto a dirt road.

Confusion creased my brow. "Where are we going?"

"I just need to stop for a bit to get something."

Get something? The large expanse of…whatever this place was—parking areas and warehouses and huge storage facilities of some kind, was empty. I knew there wasn't really anywhere safe to stop on the side of the main road we'd been on, but why was he driving so far in here? Darkness seemed to follow us the further he went in.

He left the engine idling and reached across me and into the glove compartment. "Excuse me," he said. The light from the compartment made my silvery pants shimmer, as he pulled out a pack of cigarettes.

A sickening feeling rose in my gut as he took one out and lit it.

"I thought you said you didn't smoke," I said, my voice a little shaky.

"I don't," he replied. "Only rarely, when I'm nervous, or excited."

"Nervous?" I swallowed. "Why are you nervous?"

He gave me that lingering look again as he took a few drags of the cigarette. "Well, I *am* out with a beautiful woman."

Woman? I was sixteen for Christ's sake. I'd been flattered by his compliments earlier but now I felt *flattened*. Compressed. Contained. My shoulders tensed and I tried to comprehend what was going on.

Alex stubbed the cigarette out on the dash. "That'll do, don't want to shorten my lifespan too much." He gave a laugh.

"Um, I think we should—"

I sucked in a sharp breath through my nose as his lips came crashing down on mine. They were hard, tough, strong. I leaned backward, trying to release myself from his kiss, which was nothing like a kiss should be, but he only pushed against me harder until the back of my head was pressed against the glass of the passenger side window. I grasped his shoulders and pushed, moving my head to the side to try to get a breath. He released his lips.

"Alex, stop. What are you doing?"

He relaxed. "Oh, Sasha, I'm so sorry. I just got overwhelmed with attraction for you for a moment." He shook his head and rubbed the stubble of his jaw, which on New Year's Eve I had found alluring but now found prickly and uncomfortable.

Overwhelmed? More like possessed by some unseen demon hell bent on destruction. Somehow I was making a habit of attracting bad kissing experiences, but unlike Jordan's Apoca-lips and Taylor's nicotine-filled kiss, this was worse. Because it didn't feel awkward or just plain unappealing, it felt wrong. It felt rushed, it felt dangerous.

He stroked my hand softly. "You're so beautiful. And so mature. Our emails…getting to know you…I just, I've never met anyone quite like you before." The moonlight made his eyes appear glassy as his gaze ran across my face.

If he'd said that before launching himself at me I would have smiled and blushed, inhaled a sweet, anticipatory breath. But my lips twitched and the air thickened inside the car.

"I think tonight is the perfect time to take our relationship to the next level, don't you?" He lifted his hand to my cheek and I flinched. He leaned closer and despite turning my head away, he kissed my cheek, then my lips.

My hands put pressure on his chest, but his strong body stayed where it was. "Alex, I'm not ready for that. Not yet."

Not ever. He'd ruined any chance by being so forceful.

"That's not the impression you gave me." His voice hardened. "I've been patient. I've spent time getting to know you. There's no more reason to wait."

"But—"

"Surely you knew what we'd be doing tonight, I mean, you saw who I was, you got in the car, looking all sexy. It's okay if you're nervous, I understand, but it's time. I want this, Sasha. I want *you*." His hot, needy breath swirled around my face.

A subtle trembling affected my voice box. "Ah, shouldn't we get to the restaurant? We don't want to be late for the reservation." I really just wanted to ask him to take me home, but something told me I needed to stay calm and not overreact, not upset him.

He tipped his head back and chuckled, and as the smell of cigarette smoke wafted out of his mouth and filled the car, a wave of sickness overtook me.

"Oh, Sasha, there *is* no reservation."

CHAPTER 21

My first instinct was to scream. My second was to open the door and get the hell out of the vehicle. I attempted both at once.

As my hand grabbed the door handle, his hand closed hard over my mouth. His hot, smoke-scented, angry hand, stifling my scream and half blocking off my nostrils.

"Don't do this to me, Sasha. Don't lead me on and then reject me. You can't back out now." His voice was high-pitched and urgent.

He relaxed his grip but instead of responding to his pleas I tried to scream again. His hand pressed harder against my mouth and he grunted. An annoyed, frustrated, angry grunt.

"Scream and I'll be the last face you see." His voice was sharp in my ear.

My eyes bulged beneath their sockets, my hands grappling with the door but his other hand closed over my torso, holding me in place. My chin trembled, and a heavy sense of dread and hopelessness replaced my adrenaline rush. My body relaxed and I whimpered beneath his hand. *No, no, this couldn't be happening. Not to me. Please. Please!*

"I'll remove my hand if you promise not to scream. Promise?"

I nodded furiously. It was getting hard to breathe.

He let go slightly, testing me, and I kept quiet. He removed his hand from my mouth but kept the one across my body. "You just need to relax, Sasha. I don't want to hurt you."

"But you are!" I cried. "You are! By doing this. Why? Why, Alex?" I hoped if I used his name he might lighten up a bit.

He smacked his hand across my mouth again. "Shush! What did I say before?"

Scream and I'll be the last face you see.

I realized the premonition we'd had wasn't about his sister. It was about me. I was the one in danger, he was the one who needed to be stopped.

His sister. His sister! I had to get him talking about her. I relaxed again and nodded that I understood and wouldn't scream or call out. His eyes no longer intrigued me, they terrified me. They were dark pits of evil lust that I never wanted to see again.

His hand softened and I said, "What about your sister? Why would you want to be like her husband and hurt someone? Hurt me?" My voice was quieter but pleading, desperate to find a way to get through to any part of him that may be good, that may hold hope of him realizing that this was all a big mistake and he didn't really want to hurt me. My mind was grasping at straws, but what else could I do, short of giving up?

He was silent for a moment, staring at me, and I thought I'd hit a nerve. Gotten through to him. But then he laughed. Laughed a sickening, arrogant laugh I'd never heard until tonight. It sent sharp shivers down my spine.

"Do you think the dinner reservation is the only thing I lied about? I mean, seriously, how naive are you?" He teased me with the patronizing tone of his voice, and my body shook. "I don't have a sister. I really outdid myself this time."

This couldn't be true. He'd told me all about her, my sisters and I had wanted to help her, to help this woman we didn't even know whom we believed to be in danger. And she didn't even exist? And then his words hit me harder. *This time.* This time?

"Her name was Lily. She had the same fear in her eyes. If only she'd agreed, surrendered, she'd still be here." He ran a finger across my cheekbone, his touch like a knife slicing my skin. "But you—you're feistier. You have an edge about you. That will only make this more satisfying for me." He sniggered. "C'mon, it'll be fun. I know you're attracted to me."

I clenched my jaw.

Lily. Her name *was* Lily. Had been.

He'd done this before. Whatever *this* was, and someone else hadn't been so lucky. Maybe if I *did* agree, surrendered, it wouldn't be so bad and at least I would survive. He clearly just wanted some fun. Surely he didn't really want to hurt me, or worse? A gush of vanilla aroma shot up my nose and I sucked in a breath. It overpowered the cigarette smell and his hot, sweaty skin, and I knew why the ghost Savannah had seen had not been able to speak. He'd covered her mouth too. She was like the premonition and I was the future, history repeating itself. But no. It couldn't. I couldn't let it. Couldn't give in.

I had to get away from him. Had to fight. Had to overpower him somehow, like the vanilla scent had done. I didn't know how, he was strong, but the scent had given me a sliver of hope. A tiny element of possibility. A chance to detour from the destiny that Alex's sick mind had envisioned.

"I won't fight," I said, forcing my body to relax as much as possible. "I know you're strong." I leaned back against the seat. "But please, can I ask one thing?"

He eyed me with curious suspicion.

"I've never smoked before, and I'd really like to try it. Could I, please? To help me relax?" I darted my gaze toward the glove compartment.

His eyebrows rose. "You want a cigarette?"

I nodded. "You could have another one too, I don't mind."

He chuckled, and twisted his lips to one side. "Since you're being so cooperative." He looked at the glove compartment and reached toward it, and in that flash of distraction with his hands off me, my only chance, I pushed down on the door handle and flung open the door, diving to the side with as much effort as I could.

"You bitch!" He dove after me, but most of my body was hanging out the door. My hands met with dirt and I tried to grab it, anything, to help propel myself forward. His hands were on my legs, pulling me back, but I flailed about and kicked as hard as I could so he couldn't get stability. I hoped as he leaned over to the passenger side that the gearstick was digging into his groin and causing pain. I heaved myself forward, screaming, shuffling, and wriggling as much as I could so he couldn't get a definite hold. His hand kept grabbing and releasing, grabbing and releasing, my sleek pants slippery in his grasp. One of my high heels fell off, and before the other could I turned to look at him and take aim, kicking sharply toward his head and shoving the heel of my shoe into his eye.

He let go and I assumed he grasped his face in pain, but I didn't waste time looking. I tumbled out of the car and scrambled to standing, my bare feet connecting with the ground that was cool and rough against the skin of my soles, and slightly moist. My voice did weird things, my screams and calls for help didn't make any sense, it was as though some kind of tribal warrior had possessed me. I knew he would chase me, so I had to move fast. I had to keep moving and not look back. I realized too late I was running toward the industrial yard, filled with various sized buildings and large metal containers of some kind, instead of back toward the road where I could potentially flag down a car for help. I couldn't turn back, I had to try to evade him, hide somewhere, get somewhere small he couldn't fit, anything to stop him—

"Agh!" Pain shot through my neck as my head was yanked backward. My hair twisted within his fist, my body came to a halt, and I resisted the automatic urge to cry and give up. Instead, my nerves kicked into gear, and muscle memory created a new instinct. His arm swung around my neck but before he could take hold I grabbed his forearm with both hands and yanked it down, leaning forward abruptly, his arm straightening out. I stepped my leg that was closest to him to the side, crossing it behind my other one, and twisted my body slightly, ramming my elbow hard into his groin. As he folded forward in agony, I punched him in the head and ran for it.

Take that you sick bastard!

I felt a rush of power, an energy I'd never had before, and leapt onto the nearby metal fence, hooking my toes into the gaps and climbing up and over it like I'd done it a thousand times before. I didn't know where I was going, as long as I kept going, kept moving. I had no idea if he had pulled himself together and was following me, but I ran to the narrow gap between two buildings, running through it like it was a tunnel showing me my escape route, while at the same time rummaging in my back pocket for my phone. Due to the protective cover it was hard to get out, and once I did, I slipped on the ground which was slick from the light rainfall, falling forward onto my hands and knees and dropping my phone. I winced, reaching out for my phone, and frantically got back up. I instinctively called home, realizing once I heard Savannah answer that I should have called the police first. But I wanted to hear my sister's voice, any of them. I needed my family and I needed them now.

I turned to the left at the end of the gap and leaned against the back of a metal container or dumpster nearby, panting and gasping. "Savvy! Help! It's Alex, he's trying to hurt me, he's—"

"Sasha! Where are you?"

"He drove down some dirt road, he's going to come after me, get help, quick! I think I'm at—"

My voice was cut off as a hand clamped tightly over my mouth and the other grabbed my phone. I tried to grasp his arm like before but he was in a different position. I tried to scream but only a weak, shaky murmur passed through my lips, blocked by his hand. Held in position against the metal container, my eyes widened and darted to the side where my only link to help was being held by my attacker. Alex held the phone up in front of me, taunting me, then pressed 'end call,' my hope fading along with the connection. He tossed the phone to the ground and turned me to face him, and once again I looked into those eyes of evil.

"Oh, Sasha. It could have been so perfect. Could have even made up for the accident that happened with Lily. It was her fault, silly girl. If she'd just let me have what was rightfully mine…what I had *earned*. But she went and rejected me, just like you. I thought you'd be different. But now look what you're making me do." He tightened his grip and his eyes hardened. "No one will find you here." He roughly moved me further away, down behind one of the buildings, a warehouse of some kind. In the distance there was only long, weedy grass that grew upward into the hills and trees, no sign of any houses or lights for miles.

I glared at him, the face I'd once found so alluring now so disgusting. A dirty, chemical sort of smell invaded my nose. A bitter taste rose up my throat and I gathered it all up in my mouth and spat my fury out at him.

He winced and squinted, wiping his face with his forearm. "Want to play dirty, huh?" He yanked me further along the back of the building, but not once did I surrender. I'd found the warrior within and I was not going out without a fight. My arms bent upward and held close to my chest by his strong hands, I reached for one of my ears, pretending I was hunching inward and cowering from him. I managed to extract my earring and when he put his face close to mine, trying to kiss me, I scratched his face with the hook of the earring. I knew it wouldn't be that sharp, but it was better than nothing. I would use anything and everything available to me.

He pushed my hand away and the earring dropped to the ground. "Like that's going to stop me," he said. His hands still holding mine against my chest, I clawed at him as his hot breath burned my face. I scratched his cheeks, his neck, anywhere I could, getting his DNA under my fingernails. No way was this creep going to get away with this. As my body moved backward with his unrelenting pressure against my body, I winced as my foot met with broken glass and warm blood moistened my skin. I had to get it, had to get the glass. I tried to stay still, cowering and dropping my body low, letting his body weight overpower me to the ground. He stood over me as I ended up on the ground, one of my hands breaking free and fumbling for the glass under my feet. I grasped a handful of whatever was on the ground and launched it at his leg. It sliced through his trousers and he growled like an animal. He bent over me and grabbed my wrists. "Drop it, Sasha. Drop it."

I dropped it, but spat in his face again.

"Now, get over here." He hooked his hands under my armpits and dragged me over the broken glass. I cried out as it scraped against the underside of my legs, but at the same time I was glad that my blood and DNA were being left all over the place. If worse came to worst the detectives would be able to figure out what happened, find me, bring him to justice. I hoped.

He stopped beside a low, broken brick wall that looked like it had been used as some kind of outdoor fireplace or furnace, and I almost threw up as fear spun like a cyclone in my belly. What was he planning? What was he actually going to do with me? The ground beneath me was uneven; small, hard rocks poking into my skin through my clothes, and I tried to focus on the sensations of that, instead of the sensation of him clambering on top of me as I struggled and kept trying to push him away.

As his mouth ran over mine, I bit down hard on his lip. He yelled at me and growled again. "It doesn't matter what you do, it won't be enough. You'll get tired and succumb. Me? I'm strong, I can handle more than you."

"I've handled more in my life than you'll *ever* understand," I scowled.

"Oh, like what? Your poor, weak father disappearing. Ha! I've been through worse than that."

I was no longer scared of his eyes. I stared into them with fierce contempt, showing him just how strong I was. Just how much I could handle. He may have power over me physically but he was not going to win mentally. If my life had taught me one thing it was that mental strength grew the more challenges you went through, but it also grew stronger the more love you had in your life. And by the looks of things, Alex was seriously lacking in that department. But me, I had four sisters and a mother, and even though he was gone, a father who somewhere, in some other realm, still loved me and guided me. I would not let this crazy predator take that strength away from me. I would grip it strongly inside myself, hold onto it no matter what he did, and keep my attention on that. That could never be attacked or destroyed.

Every chance I got I resisted him, pushed against him, bit him, clawed at him. He was going to be a cut up, walking bag of evidence after all this. He'd only managed to rip my top at the bottom, but the frilly bits stayed put, and as he tried to get at my pants I head-butted him. It hurt like hell but no way was I giving in.

I had no idea how much time had passed. I just knew that I had to keep trying, keep delaying things. Savannah would have called the police and Mom, and somehow they had to figure out where I was. Except my sisters thought I was going to a restaurant called Billie's. All Savannah knew was that we'd gone down a dirt road, but she would think I was in the opposite direction, not on the way to Fern Ridge.

My persistent counterattacks must have started getting on his nerves, because now he glared at me angrily. "This fun is starting to wear off," he said. "You're more challenging than I thought." He eyed me intensely. "I can't risk you getting away and telling the cops. Time for a change of strategy."

He put one hand on my right shoulder, pinning me down, and the other on my neck under my chin.

Oh God no. Please. No.

He pressed down, and my heart pounded hard against my ribcage with the need for oxygen. My free hand flailed about helplessly. I tried to remove his grip but it was too strong, I clawed again at his face but that wasn't doing anything. I looked into his eyes, trying once more to plead with him but he looked like he was on something, he barely looked human.

I didn't want his face to be the last thing I saw.

I looked away, the scent of rain dense in the air. I tried to conserve energy and hold my breath, delay the inevitable. But a scent wafted around me, between my face and his, and my eyes burned with hot tears, and probably the pressure building in my head.

Dad's cologne.

He hadn't been trying to show his approval of Alex, he'd been trying to warn me. How could I be so stupid not to think of that? But it was no use now, it was too late. Nothing could stop this.

The scent intensified and seemed to be coming from my left, behind the corner of the brick wall. Dazed and losing focus and air, I glanced to the left, and was overcome with the aroma. I knew what was happening...Dad was here. He was here, ready to meet me when I passed out and crossed over to the other side. I would get to be with him again. The man I'd lost whom I'd now found again, at least in some way. All this time, the scent had been preparing me for this, telling me that he would be here, that we would be reunited. I would finally know the secret behind his death, and that was the only thing that gave me peace, that finally allowed me to surrender to the fading oxygen levels, the pain and pressure in my skull.

Okay, Dad. I'm ready. He won. But he can't, can never, take me away from you. I'll help you once I get there, we'll get through to my sisters, your daughters, somehow, and help them find out the truth. You don't have to worry, even if you did something bad, it doesn't matter anymore.

My mind spoke my thoughts as though each word was instantaneous, everything occurring all at once, as my consciousness seemed to float in a transitory space where there was no time or space. Somehow, I knew my dad could hear my thoughts, could understand me. I could feel it, even more strongly than I could feel Alex's hand gripping my throat. The physical was fading away. It would be easy now.

Easy to succumb and let it happen, and just allow the next step to occur.

The scent intensified, and as it overtook my awareness it seemed to heighten the sense of the physical for one last moment, one last flash of the world before I left it. My blurry vision sharpened for a second, enough to notice something I hadn't seen before. To my left, just behind the corner of the brick wall, was an object. If it hadn't been for a glimpse of a memory, I wouldn't have paid attention. But the vision I'd shared with my sisters at the start of the year came rushing back. Savannah had seen a rock. This was a rock. It was just within my grasp if I could muster the strength to reach for it.

The scent seemed to emanate from it, and I realized in that brief moment, as everything seemed to be happening all at once, that Dad was not preparing for me to meet him. He was preparing me to fight. He didn't want me to give up.

Knowing it was now or never, I took that mental strength I had held onto tightly within myself and focused it into my left arm, once helpless, now filled with power. Alex's eyes were on my face, watching me die. Mine were on the rock, watching it hit his head in my mind, visualizing the outcome that I needed to survive. My shaky fingers stretched out behind the brick wall, grasping the rock, and though it felt heavier than it looked, I lifted it high. As I locked my eyes back on Alex's unsuspecting gaze, I brought the rock down against the side of his head. Hard. As hard as I could.

His eyes went blank. He collapsed on top of me, his hand relaxing on my throat and my lungs sucking in gasps of air.

I thought I heard someone call my name, but my mind

was foggy, all other senses numbed, apart from scent.

I lay there, gasping, trying to breathe, unable to move him from my body but desperate for him to get off in case he came to.

I could hear something, but couldn't make it out. All my attention and energy was focused on the pounding and rush of blood as circulation normalized in my head.

In an instant the weight above me eased, and the cool night air grazed my exposed belly, tiny raindrops tickling my skin. My vision tried to focus, but it was hard enough in the dark, let alone with what I'd just experienced. Alex lay passed out beside me, or dead for all I knew—I had no idea what my hit had done to him—and someone was on top of him, holding him down. Next thing, a hand was on my face, a gentle, soothing hand, and then arms were under me, lifting me, supporting me, taking me away from the man who'd almost taken my life.

As I glanced back at his limp body, I saw that it was Riley Pearce on top of him, holding him down with muscles clenched. Which meant…

I focused on my feet where two people held my legs as I was carried away. Savannah was one of them, her face filled with both fear and relief. Serena was on the other side, a strength in her face I hadn't seen before.

"It's okay, we've got you," said a voice from behind me. Damon Jameson. He was holding my upper body.

They lay me down again, and Damon put his jacket underneath my head. Serena took off her cardigan and laid it over my torso. Savannah put her sweater on top of my feet. She turned to check on Riley.

"He's still out," he called out. "But he has a pulse."

So I hadn't killed him. Part of me was glad. I didn't want to be responsible for killing anyone, despite what they may have done. But part of me wanted him dead, that part of me that held all the anger and fear and uncertainty about my life and what we'd been through. And I didn't want him to wake up and start attacking Riley, or all of us. Either way, it was over. The warrior within me had triumphed. The empowered goddess had claimed her right to live.

Lights flashed nearby and a siren rang out. I heard shuffling and people's voices. Someone said, "Call the paramedics." For me? Did I need medical attention? I was okay, wasn't I? I had survived. I just needed to catch my breath and I'd be fine. I tried to maneuver myself upright, but a wave of dizziness pushed me back down.

"Hey, stay still okay?" said Damon. "Help will be here soon."

A police officer crouched next to me, peering at my face and scanning my body. "I can see your neck's got some bruising coming up; where else are you hurt?"

I had no idea. Everything was a blur, I was just glad to be alive.

"It's okay, you don't have to speak, just point if you can."

I tried to look down at my body to see where my injuries were, and noticed my wrist looked different. My rose quartz bracelet, it was gone. The one Savannah had given me. "My bracelet," my voice scratched. "Where is it?" I rotated my wrist, and became aware of pain in there too where he had gripped me hard.

"Don't worry, let's just focus on tending to your wounds until the medics get here." The cop put some kind of padding on the underside of my legs which were probably still bleeding from the broken glass.

"But…I need it!" My voice struggled to become loud enough. For some reason, all I could think of was the bracelet, the comforting sense of the gemstones against my skin, the reminder that I was one of five Delta Girls and we shared an unbreakable bond. We each had a protective piece of jewelry, and the bracelet was mine.

"Hey, hey," soothed Damon. "Is this what you're looking for?" He plucked something from his pocket and held it out to me.

"Yes!" I almost cried with relief as I took hold of it.

"I found it not far from your phone," he said, holding that up too.

My phone, still intact, no broken glass, all because of the chunky, quilted, protective cover that Jordan had bought for me. *Jordan*…If only I'd gone over to him when I'd seen him at the cemetery, instead of getting in the car with Alex.

"I'll take that for you," said Serena, putting the phone safely in her pocket.

I strung the bracelet around my wrist, but the clasp wouldn't take. "I want it on," I said. My hands shook but that wasn't it. The bracelet clasp was broken. "I can't get it on!" I cried out, and then something rumbled up inside me, bubbled and boiled, and giant sobs tumbled out of me.

"Here," said Serena, "I'll take that too and we'll get it fixed, don't worry." She took the bracelet from my hands as they weakened and dropped to my side. I sobbed profusely, tears stinging my cheeks, as four people, one of whom was a stranger, patted my face, my legs, my hand, and told me everything would be okay.

CHAPTER 22

"So, how *did* you find me?" I asked, as I got up from the hospital bed the next day after being told I was being discharged.

"GoddessOfLove," said Savannah with a smile.

"Huh?" What did my password have to do with it, and how did she know it was mine?

"I figured it was yours after you acted all weird when we had that vision. And then again in the shopping center restrooms. Serena said we should try to get into your account on the app you had installed that helps you track your phone's location. Bingo."

"And you were able to find the location of my phone after I'd called you? I thought he must have broken it when he threw it on the ground."

"Rocks and stones are no match for sparkly, burgundy crimson, padded phone covers." She grinned.

Jordan probably had no idea how his novelty gift had played a role in my rescue. I would have to thank him. And

Taylor, oh my God, Taylor! I would have to explain. He was probably wondering what I was doing out with some guy, and now he would…

I must have looked concerned because Savvy said, "Don't worry, everyone knows what happened. You had some visitors this morning when you were fast asleep, so we told them to wait 'til you were home."

"How did you get to me so fast? I mean, you beat the cops and everything."

"Riley's impressive though slightly scary advanced driving skills. Oh, and remember that vision I had at the shopping center that day, about the number 12B? Well, after we found your phone, I happened to glance up and to the side, and painted on one of the warehouses was the number 12B. I went straight for it, and that's when we saw you on the ground nearby and Riley ran for the guy. It was like a signpost, showing us where you were."

"Huh. Amazing."

A moment of silence stilled us, then I checked that I wasn't leaving anything behind and gestured to the door. "Let's get out of here," I said. Savannah crooked her elbow and I hooked my arm in hers. "Thanks," I whispered. "I mean, thanks."

She leaned in and lightly connected her head with mine. "Anytime, big sis, anytime."

Mom met us in the hall along with my other sisters, and we all walked out to the parking lot, a gush of cool wind propelling us forward. Six strong women bonded by love, family, grief, and resilience.

Nothing could ever tear us apart.

• • •

I read through the cards and organized the flowers on the coffee table. Jordan's card said that I was the strongest girl he knew. He also said don't worry about what happened during the week, it's all been forgotten. Taylor had brought flowers too, but with only a small gift card attached saying 'glad you're ok.' Tamara had made cookies, and as she placed them on the table I ate two in a matter of minutes. All this was nice, and I knew how lucky I was, but nothing could erase the trauma of what I'd experienced. Flashes of the night before kept bursting into my mind and my breath would halt in my throat and my eyes would open wide, checking, making sure he wasn't still around. The psych at the hospital said it was normal, and that it would take time to process what had happened, and to let my mind do what it needed to do. 'Don't block it out,' she'd said. 'Let yourself go through the full range of emotions—anger, fear, hopelessness, regret.' I was used to living life on an emotional rollercoaster. I'd be fine, eventually. I'd just so happened to get onto a particularly scary one at this point in time and had to ride it through to the end. Up and down, around and around, side to side, climbing and falling. I just had to make sure I held on tightly.

Footsteps clicked behind where I sat on the couch and I flinched, turning my head. Amazing how quickly the brain could create a new reflex. Fear was a powerful force. "Here you go, my darling." Mom held out my rose quartz bracelet. "All fixed, courtesy of Talia's handiwork." Talia approached me alongside Mom.

I smiled my thanks and held up my bruised wrist. I could see Mom's eyes trying to glaze over from the evidence of her daughter's attack as she hooked the bracelet around my wrist. She patted my hand and then came to sit next to me. Everyone hovered for what seemed like hours—talking, reassuring, asking if I needed anything, distracting me with lighthearted topics, until I noticed Serena and Savvy whispering to each other on the other couch.

"No," Serena said, softly but loud enough for me to hear. Savannah took the laptop from Serena's lap, and she eyed me with a serious expression.

"What is it?" I asked, not sure if I wanted to know what they were looking at.

Mom went over to them and checked out the screen. Her hand flew to her chest in what appeared to be relief. So why the secrecy and caution? Mom nodded at my sisters, then carried the laptop over to me.

It was a media report just in. Alex would make a full recovery, but was being charged for my attack and attempted murder. But, the reason I knew Savannah wanted me to see it was because further down the page there was a photo of a girl, a young woman.

She had brown hair, and her name was Lily.

Alex had apparently confessed to her murder, which had been unsolved for the past seven months. It was an accident, he'd said. He hadn't meant to kill her. But when she'd tried to fight him off he did what he had to do to stop her telling anyone. Just like he would have done with me. Except with me, it was clear it would be no accident. The look in his eyes—he'd wanted to watch me die. Despite what he thought he believed, he wanted the power of taking a life, wanted that rush he'd experienced with Lily, I could tell. But it stopped with me. He wouldn't be able to hurt anyone else now. Wouldn't be able to stalk and 'groom' any other young woman to end up meeting him in person so he could live out his sick fantasies.

I glanced at Savannah with my eyebrows raised, pointing to the photo. She nodded. It must be a strange thing for her to see something, someone, in the spirit form, and then see them how they were in real life. Me, I only smelled things, it was harder to distinguish their significance, but I was getting better at using my gift day by day.

I read further into the article, clicking a link to another report on Lily's murder. Her mother had said that she still bought Lily's favorite shampoo and conditioner, vanilla scented, in order to feel close to her. I took a deep breath and sent a silent thank you to Lily, for giving me that glimmer of hope when I needed it, that push to muster up the courage and open the car door to make a dash for it. I also had Dad to thank. If it wasn't for the smell of his cologne, I wouldn't be alive right now.

"He was there," I said to no one in particular.

"What's that, sweetie?" asked Mom.

"Dad. He was with me. I could feel him."

Mom's bottom lip trembled as she gently took my hands in hers.

"You know how I told the police I picked up the rock and hit Alex? It was Dad who showed me where it was. I could smell his cologne, it made me look in that direction. I don't even know what the rock was doing there, looking back it seemed a bit out of place, like somehow, he'd put it there for me." I furrowed my brow as I recalled that surreal moment between life and death when every second mattered.

Mom's hand went to her chest again. "That's my David,"

she said, tears glossing over her eyes.

I handed the laptop back to Serena and she closed it. I thought back to how I'd managed to fight off a grown man. How amazingly, I was stronger than I thought I could ever be. But I wanted to be even stronger. I *would* be even stronger.

"Savannah?" I said, looking into my sister's eyes—eyes that saw way more than anyone could comprehend.

"Yeah?"

"Sign me up for your Taekwondo class."

A hint of a smile teased at her lips.

Mom moved closer. "Honey, it's okay. You don't need to be scared anymore; you don't need to—"

"No." I stood. "It's not about him. It's about me. I want to do this."

"Okay, cool," said Savvy. "Ninja sisters." She grinned.

I grinned back. "Just so you know, I'm going to give the rest of my New Year's resolutions the flick. Except for a new one: I'm going to train for my black belt." I held my chin high, and Savvy stood too, holding her hand up. I high-fived it then winced. "But, maybe I'll wait 'til my injuries have healed."

Savannah gave me a thumbs up and my Mom and sisters stood. We moved close together, arms embracing, and hearts lighting up with the promise of hope.

CHAPTER 23

"You sure you don't want to come in?" I heard Tamara say from the front door, as I emerged from my bedroom in the afternoon after having Monday off school.

I angled my ear toward the voices, hearing a muffled, "No, no, just tell her I hope she likes the muffins."

I quickly walked to the door. "Hi, Jordan."

"Oh, hi. I was just leaving. Thought you might need to rest." He had half stepped off the porch.

"No, I'm good." I glanced at the tray of muffins in Tamara's hands. "Chocolate chip?"

"And some have white chocolate too, in case you like them. My mom wasn't sure so she made two batches."

My heart warmed. He was so genuine. Some guys would pretend they made the muffins themselves, or bought them from a gourmet bakery, rather than revealing his mommy made them. But not Jordan. What you saw was what you got. And that, I now knew, was a very admirable trait to possess.

"Please thank her for me. And thank you, too." I wanted

to thank him for more than the muffins; for forgiving me for the horrendous nickname and for visiting me in the hospital even though he couldn't come in the room to see me, and for buying me the phone cover that inadvertently helped my sisters and their boyfriends come to my rescue. But I couldn't think about all of that right now, couldn't talk about it right now. But muffins...muffins I could handle.

"I, um, that night, when I saw you. I wasn't following you or anything, I had just been going for a walk when I noticed you. I didn't want to get in the way, so I hid behind the tree. I guess I was curious too. If I'd known who he was, I would have..." He hung his head. "I wish..."

"Jordan, it's okay," I said.

He eyed me with an apology that wasn't necessary. "Anyway, I'll leave you to it," he said. "See you when you're back at school."

I nodded and smiled, and he waved a little as he walked off, almost tripping on the plants lining the pathway to our door. I smiled some more.

"One or two?" asked Tamara, practically salivating at the goodies in her hands.

"Are you asking for me or yourself?" I chuckled.

"You of course! These are for you, not me."

"Um, I think there are *plenty* to share around, I don't need to eat *all* of them."

Tamara's eyes brightened. "So you don't mind if I try one?"

"One? I'm thinking two." I winked, and she laughed.

We sat down to eat the muffins, which were still warm from Mrs. Davis' oven, and when I was about to reach for a second helping, there was a knock at the front door.

"Maybe Jordan's mom has made a third batch?" Tamara joked.

I gave her a light whack on the arm as she stood to answer the door.

"Sasha around?"

Taylor.

I stood, smoothed down my top and went to the door. "Hi."

"Hi." His eyes scanned me, looking for my wounds. "Are you okay?"

I shrugged. "As okay as I can be." Physically at least. I still had regular counseling sessions to mentally prepare for. I wasn't looking forward to revisiting the night of the attack, but I knew it was a necessary evil to be able to move forward.

He grasped my arms, and for a moment I tensed.

"Sorry, does that hurt?"

"No, it's okay."

It just reminds me of being grabbed by him, that's all. No biggie, no biggie at all.

"I'm so glad you're safe. I couldn't believe it when I heard." Taylor let go of my arms and ran a hand through his wavy hair.

"Taylor, it's okay. It's all over now, he's going to get what he deserves."

"And you had actually been communicating with him? Before all this?"

I stepped outside, the low afternoon sun causing me to squint and cover my eyes. I closed the door behind me to give us privacy and stepped to the side of the porch. "I thought he was you," I whispered.

Taylor screwed up his nose. "But why didn't you

say something?"

Boys. They were so oblivious sometimes. "I dropped hints. And I just thought you would deny it anyway, as you'd—*he'd*—said he would do if I ever asked you outright."

"I wish I'd known." He looked away. "And so when you met him, thinking you were going to meet up with me, you just went with him? Just like that?" he asked. "Were you all dressed up? I mean, you always look great, but were you wearing something, you know…" he moved his hands about, as though to indicate something curvy.

My mouth gaped. "What? What's that got to do with anything! He had this planned from the start; it had nothing to do with what I was wearing. Do you think I asked for it, is that it?" I planted my hands on my hips, my chest burning with anger.

"Hey, hey, no of course not." He grasped my arms again but I pushed them away. "That's not what I meant. I'm sorry, I guess I'm just trying to understand how it all happened, it made me feel so awful that I wasn't around to help you."

The guy looked genuinely troubled. I relaxed my body. "It's okay, it's been hard for everyone to process."

"Sasha," he spoke softly, then moved in close. "Come here." He slid his arms gently around my back, pulling me in for a hug. I accepted, and slid my arms around his back too. I felt smaller though, beneath his embrace, like it was making me shrink. After a moment he pulled back a little, then cupped his hand around my cheek, looking into my eyes. He leaned forward and kissed me softly. It was over before it had begun, as I turned my head to the side.

"Taylor, wait." I held my hand between our faces.

"What is it?"

"I'm not, I don't." I nibbled at my bottom lip. The last thing I wanted right now was a kiss. Even from him, even from the guy I'd so wanted to continue kissing on New Year's Eve, and who had promised to give up smoking for me before I would let him kiss me again. But it felt different now. Things *were* different now.

"Sorry, I shouldn't have done that I guess. I just thought, I wanted to make it up to you, to make you feel better."

I eyed him curiously.

He lowered his head and shook it. "Oh, man."

I crossed my arms and waited for him to speak the words that seemed to be teetering on the edge of his lips.

"I lied, Sasha. I'm sorry. I wasn't going to help my parents with business stuff on Friday night." He looked up and our eyes connected. "I went to a party. It was just a small thing, at Samantha's house. She invited me and I didn't want to say no. I thought it would be harmless, but decided not to tell you as I thought you'd be upset with me going to another girl's house."

"So while I was feeling guilty about going out with Alex, who I thought was you, you weren't even where you'd told me you'd be?"

"Sorry. But hey, we're even now. I mean, you didn't text me or anything to tell me your plans that night."

"Even?" My eyes widened. "Even?" I jabbed my finger at his chest. "If my plans had gone to plan, I would have told you later that I'd been out with Alex, and I certainly wouldn't have let anything happen between me and him had he been a normal guy, but no way in hell are we even! While I was fighting for my life you were partying with friends, and a girl who probably has the hots for you!" My insides churned with a bitter sensation.

"I didn't mean it that way!"

"You're making a habit of saying things the wrong way then. And Samantha does have the hots for you, doesn't she? But I guess you're going to tell me you didn't let anything happen between you so it doesn't really matter, right?"

He looked at me blankly.

"Right?"

Silence. I ran a hand through my hair. "Oh great, so you what, like, kissed or something?"

"She kissed me, I swear. Eventually I told her it had to stop."

"Eventually?"

"Well it all happened so fast, it took me a minute to get my head straight, but once I did I knew I wanted to be with you, not her. I wanted us to have our proper kiss, without the cigarettes."

I shook my head. How had this conversation turned so sour? Barely three days ago, I was preparing to leave this crazy, unpredictable world, and now here I was arguing with my sort of boyfriend about a girl he sort of kissed? I didn't have the patience for all this. I didn't want the drama. I just wanted simple. Simple, easy, honest, genuine. No lies, no facades, no secrets.

"Taylor, thanks for dropping by, and for the card. I really appreciate it. But I can't deal with this."

"I'm sorry, it's okay. I should have waited a bit longer for you to recover. Don't worry, we can talk about this another time." He patted my arm.

"No, you don't get it. I can't deal with this. With us. The secrets, the uncertainty, the whole..." I waved my hands around "…scattered chaos of everything. I have enough of that in my life." I looked him in the eye. "Sorry to leave you hanging, and thanks for making the effort with the smoking and all, but I think we should just stay friends."

"Friends? Wait, Sasha, but what about…" His face creased as he searched his mind for the right words.

"I think you're a great guy, I do, but I just don't think you're great for me."

There, I said it. I realized then that I had put him on a pedestal, one he probably didn't belong on. He wasn't a bad guy, he just had a few things to learn along his journey. And I was further ahead, further along in my journey, and heading in a different direction. The more I progressed, the more I knew I had wanted to be with the *idea* of him, rather than the *actual* him.

He gave a resigned nod. "Okay then."

"Okay."

"Okay." He turned away, then back again. "I really am glad you're safe." Then he walked off, and before I went back inside, I watched him for a little while, mentally saying goodbye to that part of me that had wanted him so badly, and promising myself I wouldn't ever settle for second best. As Taylor went to turn around the corner and into his street, he pulled something from his pocket, and even after he'd disappeared from Roach Place, a sinuous wave of smoke from his cigarette was left behind like a ghost.

CHAPTER 24

"Everything okay?" Mom asked, as I went to go into my bedroom and found her coming out of it.

"Yep. I just need to be alone for a while."

"Okay, well I've just changed your sheets, so you have a nice fresh bed for tonight." She smiled and scurried off to the kitchen. "I'll let you know when dinner is ready."

"Thanks." My voice was so quiet she probably didn't hear me. Tamara and Mom's voices traveled softly through the walls, though I couldn't understand what was being said, and Savannah and Serena were out back, apparently working on something I wasn't allowed to look at just yet. Talia was in her room, probably meditating, or making something, or generally worrying about everything and everyone. Time alone in this house was precious, and though I wanted nothing more than to be close to my family after my ordeal, I now craved some alone time.

I closed the bedroom door and sat on my bed, welcoming the soft but firm stability underneath me. My eyes scanned the room in its stillness, everything exactly where it had been on Friday before I'd gone out, yet irrevocably changed, different, somehow. But it was just my perception that had changed. My vision was clearer, my awareness stronger. I wouldn't hide behind anything anymore. I wouldn't brush aside challenges in favor of taking the easy way out. I wouldn't shy away from experiencing the full spectrum of emotions, warts and all. Life was about being honest and open, and not being afraid to be yourself.

Hang on. Something *was* different about the room.

My gaze honed in on my bedside table. An envelope was there, sitting crisply in waiting, as though tense and eager to be opened. I picked it up and slid my finger under the seal. A post-it was stuck to a crumpled piece of paper. It read:

Found this under your mattress, thought you might want to keep it. ~ Mom. P.S – You're a natural.

I folded open the paper. It was my unfinished poem about Dad.

I bit my lip. I hadn't meant for Mom to find it and read it. I hoped it hadn't upset her. I had almost forgotten about it completely, but as I read over what I had written, I was glad I hadn't thrown it out. Glad she had found it and recognized its value.

"No more unfinished business," I said to myself. "I might not be able to get closure on what happened to you yet, but I can finish this. For you," I said to Dad.

I opened my bedside drawer and got out a pen, held it poised over the paper, waiting for the right words to come. And then my fingers became cold as I noticed the pen I was holding. I gasped.

Alex's gift.

I stood abruptly, the pen stuck in my shaking hand. I saw his face, saw his eyes, saw his hand over my mouth. With each image that flashed in my mind, my breath quickened, sharpened, became louder. Until my built up emotions boiled over and came out in one angry scream.

I threw the pen against the wall. It made a light, high-pitched sound then fell to the floor. I picked it up and pulled it apart, broke it to pieces, tears streaming down my face. I then remembered Savannah's uncertain face as she'd seen the pen when I got it in the mail, and realized she must have recognized it from her vision when I'd thrown it. She hadn't wanted to disrupt my moment of happiness at receiving a gift, knowing that something down the track would cause me to want to destroy it.

Talia came rushing in, followed by Mom and Tamara. They tried to hold me steady, but still I clawed at the pen like I had clawed at Alex's face, grunting and yelling in effort. When the pen was a pathetic pile of tiny components, Mom took them from me and told Tamara to go put them in the trash. I turned to my mother and buried my face in the crook of her neck, allowing her soft skin and soothing words to absorb my tears and pain, until my body had released all it needed to release and I was left feeling lighter.

I don't know how long she stood there holding me, but I would never tire of her embrace. Whenever things got tough, or I felt alone, I would remember this moment, this unwavering, unconditional, honest embrace. She didn't try to distract me, or take away my feelings, she simply let me feel them, release them, in all their ugly glory. She knew what it was like. She knew what pain was; she had carried it on her shoulders for years, while trying to stay strong and dependable for the five of us girls. She stayed put, until I told her I would be okay. She didn't hover, or fuss over me, she simply asked if I wanted to be left alone again, and I nodded. Then she softly closed the door behind her after my sisters had walked out.

Before I looked at the poem again, I took out my phone and opened up my blog. My instinct had been to delete the whole thing, tainted by modernprophet's comments, but the police had wanted it for evidence and some educational program about predators. They had also asked for the emails we'd exchanged, which was kind of embarrassing as they were personal, but in the scheme of things it didn't matter. If it helped Alex get what he deserved, and helped educate others to look out for the signs if the same thing happened to them, then it would be worth it.

So I wrote a blog post, advising my subscribers that this would be my last post. At the end of it, I wrote:

> *I will still make goals, I will still strive for achievement and accomplishment, just not in public. If you want to keep updated on my progress in life, and my scentsational entrepreneurial adventures, you can ask me how I'm doing— face to face. I'm taking a break from online stuff for a little while, and those of you who I know personally and are my friends, I look forward to seeing you soon.*
>
> *P.S.—One last resolution for the road…I'm going to get a black belt in Taekwondo. If you see a girl walking down the street with burgundy crimson hair, a lipstick-coated smile on her face, smelling of Fresh Fruity Blast, and wearing white clothing and a black belt—that'll be me.*
>
> *Watch out world, Sasha version 2.0 is coming…*

I grinned as I hit 'publish,' then was just about to share the link on Facebook when I realized that all my recent posts had been set to 'public,' instead of only 'friends.' I had forgotten to adjust it each time I posted my blog links. Alex must have kept an eye on my profile and when he'd seen that I'd posted about my Mom going out on Friday to a costume party, he must have thought that would be a perfect opportunity to ask me out. I swirled a sour taste around in my mouth. Then I swallowed. No, no more. I'd had enough of him hijacking my thoughts. He was not going to spoil my newly hopeful mood. And he was not going to get in the way of what I wanted to do next.

I put my phone on my bedside table and picked up the poem, and a different pen. All I had to do was change one word at the end, and add the final line…

Where did he go? Where is he now?
We need to find the answers but don't know how
What good is a vision if we are blind?
What purpose is foresight if truth we can't find?
Somewhere he lays, but where, where?
Hidden away, I fear we'll never get there
But fear can't win, it mustn't, it ~~won't~~ will not
Somehow I'll persist, I'll find your resting spot.

CHAPTER 25

Two Days Later...

Well, I did it. Got through my first day back at school, even though Mom tried to get me to stay home. I was sick of hanging about, thinking about everything, and needed to get back to some sort of normality.

As I got my things from my locker and turned around, I noticed Jordan standing by the doorway that led outside. He was hesitating, and seemed to be pretending to check in his bag for something. I knew that, because sometimes Serena did the same thing when she didn't want to look awkward while standing around waiting. I walked over to him and smiled.

"How was your day?" he asked.

"All good. I guess." I brushed my hair from my face. "It was a distraction at least."

"Want another distraction? Or to talk? Whatever you feel like." He gestured outside. "I could walk you home if you want. I mean, if you want to walk by yourself, or with your sisters, I understand. So, I can just—"

"Sure, I'd love to." I nodded. "Actually, maybe we can walk down to the beach?"

Jordan's eyebrows rose like he wasn't expecting me to agree, let alone suggest we go somewhere. I needed to be near the water, feel the endless ebb and flow of the ocean and remember that life always moved on. And I wanted to thank him.

"Sounds good." He smiled and stepped aside for me to exit. I saw Taylor standing outside talking to Samantha. She was laughing. I wondered if he was asking her out to have fish and chips at the harbor. I bet she didn't mind cigarette smoke and wouldn't make him agree to a three-week-no-kiss challenge.

"So," he said, swinging his arms back and forth. "Miss Weir's eyes, is it just me or do they make you think of little bugs? I'm not trying to be mean, I just get these random thoughts in my head sometimes." He scratched his head. "I probably sound crazy. Sorry. I should be quiet and let you talk."

I laughed. I knew crazy and he wasn't it. In fact, I bet if I told him about the Delta Girls right now he would probably be totally okay with it. But I wouldn't tell him. Not unless I had to. And I hoped there would be no drama or crisis affecting him or his family that would require me to tell him. Hopefully what I'd been through over the weekend would be enough drama for a while. I needed simplicity right now.

"You can keep talking. In fact, I've often thought the

same thing. About her eyes."

"No way, really?"

"Yes way. I mean, they're so beady. And does she ever actually blink? It's like she just stares with her eyes open all the time. I bet she doesn't even close them when she sleeps."

Laughter shot from Jordan's mouth. "And sometimes when I look at them, it feels like they could even jump out all of a sudden. Like little bug ninjas."

I laughed again. "And her hair, what about her hair?"

"I know. You could scrub a greasy cooking pot with it. Who needs steel wool?"

We walked along in hysterics. This was exactly what I needed. Good, silly, crazy fun!

"And, and…" I struggled for breath, laughing so much, "Once, I even imagined there were little bugs trapped in her hair, and, and…" I slapped my thigh, "they tried to escape, like it was a maze or something, and one of them jumped off her head and got impaled by a split end!"

"Ha!" Jordan had to stop and fold over he was laughing so much.

"God, we're so mean," I said. "It's not her fault she has wiry, curly hair. Then again, she could at least use *some* hair product to tame them a bit." I held up my thumb and forefinger.

"Oh well, it's not like we're being that mean, we're just messing around. She *is* a good teacher, but sometimes you've gotta laugh at silly things hey?"

"Exactly." My face flushed a little. "But maybe I went a bit overboard with, um…"

"With my nickname?"

I lowered my head. "Yeah."

"Really, it's okay," he said. "I'm over it. Anyway, it *is* actually kinda funny." He smiled as I managed to glance sideways at him. "Actually, it's genius. You have a way with words."

"Oh, stop it, you. You're just being nice because I'm…" I made quotes with my fingers in the air, "fragile, at the moment."

"No I'm not. I would have stopped sulking later that Friday night anyway. I knew you didn't really mean to hurt me. You were just in shock after the ankle situation. I don't blame you. In fact, if you hadn't thought of it I probably would have called myself Apoca-lips."

"Oh you would not have!"

"Would too!"

I gave him a light slap on the arm.

"And Sasha, you're not fragile. You're strong. Remember that."

"Thanks. And thanks again for the card. And the muffins."

He waved his hand at my thanks.

Before I knew it we were on the beach, walking across the sand, our shoes still on. "Thanks for getting me that phone cover, Jordan. I don't know if you know, but it actually helped me that night."

"It did? How?"

"Well," I took a deep breath, calming myself at the memories. "He threw my phone to the ground. I thought it would have smashed. He probably thought so too. But it didn't. And Savannah and my sisters were able to track my phone's location online so they could find me. If it had broken, I don't know if the tracking would have worked.

So thanks."

"Wow," he replied. "I'm glad. But it was just coincidence, no need to thank me."

"It wasn't coincidence," I said. "It was fate."

"Fate?"

"Yeah. And maybe you moving here, that was fate too."

"How so?"

I stopped, and turned to face him. All of a sudden my confusion from the last few weeks dissipated, and everything became clear. I'd wanted the intrigue of Alex, before I knew his real motives, and I'd wanted the idea of Taylor. But, in reality, what I'd wanted all along was Jordan. "So we could try again. Erase that awkward memory, create a new one."

His large, round eyes looked in mine. This time he didn't look awkward or uncomfortable, he looked as certain as I felt. "Well, you know, I do actually have a New Year's resolution I've yet to fulfill."

"Oh, really? Are you going to start a blog?"

"Haha, no. This one is a private one." He leaned closer to me. "For your ears, eyes, and…lips, only."

My heart fluttered a little, enough to let me know I wanted this. And that this time, we would get it right.

Jordan diverted his gaze to just beyond my shoulder. "Doesn't look like there are any stray bricks lying around."

I giggled.

"But oh, hang on, what's this?" He leaned over and picked something up. "A shell." He tossed it toward the ocean. "Just in case. That could have been dangerous."

"Yeah, lucky you saw it."

He chuckled, then his face turned more serious, genuine, focused. "One step at a time," he said. "First, this."

He stroked my cheek gently with his hand. "And this." He tucked a strand of hair behind my ear.

"And this," I added, sliding my hands around his waist.

"And this." He slid one hand around my back and the other around the back of my head, so softly it was like a feather. "And…"

He leaned forward, his face coming closer to mine and darkening the afternoon sun behind him, like a solar eclipse. Or an *ec-lips*? I resisted the desire to suggest my joke. We'd had enough humor for one day, and it was time for something real, raw, and beautiful.

His lips cushioned mine, and they kissed me with the perfect balance of pressure and softness. Not too soft, not too hard, nothing like before. Just right. And I felt it throughout my whole body, the tingling, the bliss, the warmth. This was what I had been waiting for. This was what was right for me.

I would need to take it slowly, to test the waters, but I knew Jordan would be patient with me. We were, first and foremost, friends, and that was the perfect start to a relationship. The perfect start-over to my new year. A lot had happened in such a short time, but as far as I was concerned, this was my new year, starting now. The last few weeks could fade away into the past. I was only interested in the now, and the future. And right now, I was having the most perfect kiss of my life, and I couldn't be happier. And, I knew, I just knew, that Dad would have liked Jordan too.

• • •

When I'd walked home with Jordan and he declined my offer to come over, stating that he wanted to let me take my time with everything, I went inside and found Savannah standing in the living room with a big smile on her face.

"What?" I asked.

My other sisters were smiling too, except Serena who would be at her violin lesson, and Mom was home early. "Have a look in your room."

"Your room, I mean, *my* room? Since when is it my room?"

"Okay, *our* room. But look above your bed."

With curiosity I went into our room and looked above the bed. I stepped back to take it in. "Wow. Did you do this?"

"We all did a bit of it," said Savvy. "For you."

It was one of Mom's mandala paintings. The ones that came printed onto a wooden board for people to paint and fill in themselves. It was bright and colorful, filled with varying shades of my favorite color, purple, as well as pinks and reds, silver and blues—a whole explosion of beautiful colors and shapes, as though it was a visual representation of my favorite scents too: all combined.

"Aw, thanks you guys. It's so gorgeous." I smiled wide. "I love it." I turned to my sisters and hugged them. Mom slid her arm around my waist. This afternoon was turning out to be the perfect antidote to last weekend.

The front door clicked open. We all went back out to the living room.

"Did she like it?" asked Serena.

"I sure did. I do," I said. "Thanks."

"I didn't do much, my art skills aren't as good as the others," she said. "But I did have a say in the mathematical distribution of which colors should go where."

"Well it paid off," I replied. Serena took her bag and violin case to the room and returned a moment later.

"So, Savvy, Riley coming over for dinner tonight?" asked Mom.

I turned to look at my youngest sister, but she didn't reply.

"Savvy?" Mom said.

She was frozen to the spot, staring out the window. Savannah moved slowly toward it, stepping cautiously as though she might tread on a bomb.

"What is it, what do you see?" Serena asked.

Her last few steps were quick, as she rushed to the window and pressed her palms desperately against the pane of glass. Her mouth opened, her eyes were wide, and a whisper floated from between her lips. "Dad?"

CPSIA information can be obtained at www.ICGtesting.com
Printed in the USA
BVOW08s1400060316

439271BV00004B/123/P